COSIMA

Unfortunate

FOILS A FRAUD

Books by Laura Noakes

COSIMA UNFORTUNATE STEALS A STAR
COSIMA UNFORTUNATE FOILS A FRAUD

COSIMA
Unfortunate
FOILS A FRAUD

LAURA NOAKES

Illustrated by Flavia Sorrentino

HARPERCOLLINS
CHILDREN'S BOOKS

First published in the United Kingdom by
HarperCollins *Children's Books* in 2024
HarperCollins *Children's Books* is a division of HarperCollins*Publishers* Ltd
1 London Bridge Street
London SE1 9GF

www.harpercollins.co.uk

HarperCollins*Publishers*
Macken House, 39/40 Mayor Street Upper
Dublin 1, D01 C9W8, Ireland

1

ISBN 978–0–00–857935–7

Laura Noakes and Flavia Sorrentino assert the moral right to be identified
as the author and illustrator of the work respectively.

A CIP catalogue record for this title is available from the British Library.

Typeset in Weiss Std 11pt/18pt
Printed and bound in the UK using 100% renewable electricity
at CPI Group (UK) Ltd

MIX
Paper | Supporting
responsible forestry
FSC™ C007454

This book contains FSC™ certified paper and other controlled
sources to ensure responsible forest management.

For more information visit: www.harpercollins.co.uk/green

This one's for my brother Tom, for being my first and forever best friend and because I haven't written a character based upon him yet. I hope having a whole book dedicated to you makes up for this egregious oversight!

Cosima

Pearl

Diya

Mary

The Amazing Luminaire

Edmund

Miss Meriton

Miss Fox

Cat

Miles

THE LONDON GAZETTE

12th March 1900 Price 2d

WHERE WILL THE SPECTRE STRIKE NEXT?
FEARS GROW ABOUT MASTER THIEF'S NEXT TARGET

*Police on the trail of the infamous crook have urged the great
and the good to lock away valuables and secure their properties.
The Spectre has struck across multiple countries, committing a
number of high-profile thefts and leaving no clues but a small card
bearing his name. Last spring, a priceless diamond necklace that
once belonged to Marie Antoinette was taken from the Louvre
in Paris. In the summer, a Stradivarius violin was stolen from a
private residence in Berlin. And at the close of last year, the bandit
swiped a one-of-a-kind timepiece during the Gladwell–Asher Ball.
Detectives seem flummoxed by this string of offences and are no
closer to uncovering the serial burglar's identity.*

The world's greatest travelling fair in London for the first time . . .
THE AMAZING LUMINAIRE'S SPECTACULAR NOW OPEN AT EARL'S COURT, SOUTH KENSINGTON

EXPERIENCE *impossible illusions with the king of magic.*

*Be **DAZZLED** by the Clockwork Carousel, the Great Wheel
and many more thrilling rides.*

MARVEL *at amazing acrobatics, spine-tingling seances
and incredible feats of strength performed by sensational
strongman, Gustav the Mighty.*

*And see a **MASTERPIECE OF ART**, soon to be the world's most*

valuable painting:

THE LADY INVALID.

Price: ONE SHILLING & SIXPENCE.

Open 11.30 a.m. till 11.30 p.m. daily.

Must close 15th March.

NEXT DESTINATION: Prague.

PREPARATIONS UNDERWAY FOR

THE MIDNIGHT MASQUERADE

There is a tremendous stir in fashionable circles as the most
anticipated event of this year approaches this coming Friday,
16th March. The Midnight Masquerade, a lavish invitation-only
costume ball organised by Sir Theodore Vincent, concludes at
midnight, marking the end of the Spectacular's visit to London.
Earl's Court will play host to England's most distinguished
residents, with royalty, aristocrats and society figures expected
to attend and don costumes paying homage to heroes and
heroines, past, present and fictional. All proceeds of the party are
intended to benefit the city's poor.

WHAT NEXT FOR AGATHA DE LA DULCE?
GLOBETROTTING LADY REPORTER RETURNS TO ENGLAND

Our very own lady reporter has been welcomed home with a champagne reception after her record-breaking trip around the world came to a close last week. Miss de la Dulce is well known for exposing the criminality of aristocrats, revealing the injustices faced by matchbox girls and championing unfortunate children. When asked what investigation she would be pursuing next, the roving newswoman played coy . . .

CHAPTER ONE

Cosima grinned into the star-sprinkled night as she read the front page of the *London Gazette* for the thousandth time since that morning. The newspaper was now sporting a rather violent-looking jam splodge (courtesy of Cos's delicious afternoon tea) and some of the ink had smudged in dreary grey swirls (courtesy of Cos's excessive rereading) but, as she scanned the article in question yet again, a reverential shiver trailed up her back.

The Spectre. The greatest thief since – well, since Cos and her friends had pulled off the Treasure Palace Heist last year. The only difference was that nobody had thought to give *them* a glamorous nickname when five jewels suddenly vanished from the Empire Exhibition. Cos frowned, thinking of a suitable moniker that could rival the Spectre's. The

Phenomenal Pilferers? The Tremendous Thieves?

She sighed. She would have to consult Diya. Then she shook the thought away. The fact that they – four disabled girls and a wayward magician-slash-thief – were responsible for one of the most perplexing criminal mysteries of the last year was a secret they would all have to keep forever.

Whoever the Spectre was, he *definitely* wanted his exploits to be noticed; he was currently the most famous criminal in the world. There was a funny sort of ache deep in Cos's chest – a mixture of admiration and jealousy. She thought of the many crumpled newspapers stuffed down the side of her bed:

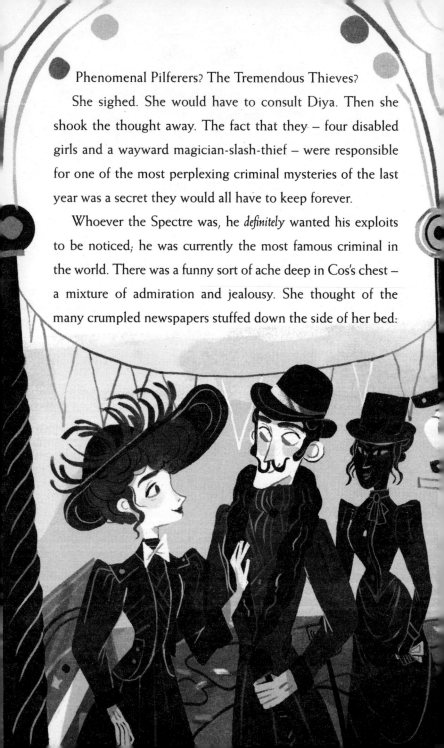

the ones with headlines that screamed *STAR DIAMOND TIARA STILL MISSING* and *COLONIAL OFFICE SEEKS VANISHED JEWELS*. They were her secrets, hidden even from her friends, who she knew regarded last year's caper as a one-off.

'Can I put the lantern down yet, Cos?' asked Dolly. 'My arm is aching something awful, and as I've only got one hand to begin with . . .'

Cos nodded, muttering an apology as Dolly hung the Luminous Lantern back on Diya's wheelchair handles.

Carefully, Cos folded the *Gazette* and slid the newspaper into her pocket.

There was a distant clap of thunder. A cool breeze sprang up as the sky darkened, and in a swirl of purple and grey storm clouds, dusk took hold. Cos pulled her raincoat close and wished the drizzle away.

A large group of girls from the Star Diamond Home were finally nearing the front of the snaking queue outside the entrance of a travelling fair, all wearing pastel-coloured uniforms that were unsuited to the awful spring weather. Cos gripped her trusty walking stick tightly as scores of elegantly dressed ladies and be-hatted gentlemen waited alongside them, wrinkling their noses and whispering when they spotted the throng of children with wheelchairs, walking sticks and ear trumpets.

Tonight, she was far too excited to care.

High above her, a twinkling sign that read

THE SPECTACULAR,

pierced the soggy gloom. Beyond the sign hundreds of lights, strung across each amusement ride and fairground stall, glowed golden. There was a hum in Cos's ears.

'Electricity,' breathed Diya, 'is utterly wonderful.'

Beside Cos, Mary clutched the illustrated map of the Spectacular that had been handed out as they joined the queue of excited visitors. Mary loved nothing more than a detailed plan where everything was just so. Plotting out possibilities helped her manage panic whirlwinds, a symptom of her hysteria. 'There are so many rides!' she said, taking out her pen and beginning to make notes on the map. 'We'll have to manage our time well if we're to see *all* the attractions.'

On Cos's other side, Pearl inked a crimson-striped fairground wagon across her palm. It joined the gleaming amusement rides, the fluttering canvas of the tents and the illuminated Great Wheel already painted up her forearm. Cos knew that Pearl was a kaleidoscope of brilliance. Her friend found some noises and smells impossible to bear, preferred to not make eye contact with other people and created the most wondrous artwork Cos had ever seen. She was never without her paintbrush.

'I can't wait to see the art,' muttered Pearl dreamily as she added a finishing flourish to an acrobat cartwheeling across her wrist. 'Can you imagine – *someone like us*, painted into a portrait?'

Two weeks before, Pearl had burst into the dormitory, the evening edition of the *London Gazette* clasped tightly to her chest. Too excited to explain, she had held up the front page:

RARE PAINTING TO GO ON SALE
THE LADY INVALID WOWS ART WORLD

London's leading art dealers Vincent & Sons are delighted to announce that their newly acquired portrait by Ambrose van Hackenboeck will go on auction this spring. The painting is expected to sell for an astronomical sum, and will be on display at the Spectacular during its London residency.

The Lady Invalid is a half-length artwork by Van Hackenboeck, one of the leading Dutch artists of the 17th century, famed for his portraits of society hostesses, gentry and royalty. This painting shows an infirm gentlewoman, bed-bound and convalescent. Like Da Vinci's **Mona Lisa**, *the identity of this most unusual sitter is unknown.*

Sir Theodore Vincent, son of the firm's founder, has long been a champion of bringing beauty to the uneducated masses. A patron of the Spectacular, he has ensured that – alongside the more frivolous entertainment on offer at the event – art has been given centre stage. The Van Hackenboeck is being exhibited in a purpose-built Picture Palace with other beautiful paintings.

Van Hackenboeck was one of Pearl's favourite artists, but the real reason she was so delighted was because of *who* he had painted: a disabled person. She had talked of almost nothing else since, her anticipation thrumming through the entire home.

'It will be an entertaining *and* educational evening out,' said Miss Meriton, dragging Cos back to the present. 'The perfect distraction from my preparations for this week's inspection.'

Miss Meriton had only recently become the matron of the Star Diamond Home, where Cos and all her friends lived. Before, the girls had lived under the gin-soaked, penny-pinching thumbs of Miss and Mr Stain, but when the siblings' cruelty and financial mismanagement were uncovered by Cos's friend and lady journalist extraordinaire, Agatha de la Dulce, they were hauled off to jail. After the Stains' departure, the Inspectorate of Children's Institutions had, for the first time in Cos's life, decided to scrutinise the care that the girls were being given. Cos wasn't worried. Miss Meriton was like a mug of hot cocoa on a gloomy day, and the improvements she had made to the Home were incredible. But the Inspectorate had asked her to fill out reams of paperwork in anticipation of their visit, and Miss Meriton had spent most of the last week bent over her desk, bags under her eyes the colour of a storm.

Cos sighed. 'I just wish Aggie could've come with us. She would have loved this.'

The matron's eyes twinkled with mischief as she gave Cos's arm a gentle squeeze. Miss Meriton and Agatha were the best of friends, and when Aggie wasn't midway through an investigation they spent all their time together. 'You never know, she might be *just* out of sight.'

The Spectacular had appeared just as the Christmas decorations had been packed away in the attic, bringing some much-needed magic to a dull January. Playbills had been pasted on every lamp post and shop shutter, announcing its arrival – and its star illusionist, the Amazing Luminaire. Overnight, countless red-and-gold striped tents sprang up, and soon spotting the latest attractions being transported into Earl's Court became a kind of sport that sent excited whispers buzzing through Kensington.

It was much more than the average fairground – even though it had carousels, waltzers and stalls aplenty. There was also a magnificent theatre tent, a thrilling switchback railway and the Picture Palace, where priceless artwork would be displayed, including *The Lady Invalid*. And, for the first time ever, the girls of the Star Diamond Home were able to join in with the excitement instead of being locked up in their dormitory.

Diya, who was a prodigious inventor and engineer, was especially excited to see all the innovations on display at the Spectacular. Cos was half convinced that Diya's brain was a state-of-the-art machine of cogs and rivets, powered by her beloved electricity. Diya's latest idea had been inspired by Pearl's love of fireworks, but her hatred of loud, unexpected bangs. She and Miles had been working together on creating silent fireworks, but it wasn't going entirely to plan, judging by the number of small fires the inventor had put out over the last few weeks.

Diya pivoted her wheelchair to get a glimpse of the fancy mechanical gates at the grand entrance. They allowed the patrons to enter one at a time, after their tickets had been checked by an attendant sitting in a brightly painted booth.

'They're called turnstiles,' she said excitedly as the fixed horizontal metal arms whirred to let in a young lady in a feathered hat ahead of them. 'They're a revolutionary invention.' Her eyes sparkled, face bright, and then – in an instant – her face fell. Diya reversed her wheelchair abruptly.

'OWWWW!' Miles yelled, clutching his foot. 'What was that for?'

Cos craned her neck, peering towards the entrance. The barrel-chested ticket attendant's gaze was fixed on Diya's wheelchair, his eyes narrowed. Cos, like every other disabled person, immediately knew the meaning behind that look.

Before Cos could tug on Miss Meriton's sleeve, the glaring attendant politely ushered the group ahead of them through the turnstiles, exited his booth and stepped towards Miss

21

Meriton, blocking them from the Spectacular. 'I'm afraid we can't allow *these* children in,' he boomed, eyes flickering coldly over the group of girls.

Sniggers and whispers spread through the queue behind them, echoing in Cos's ears.

The attendant cleared his throat, as if he were an actor on a stage, and spoke so loudly that the entire street could hear his words. 'Unfortunates are *prohibited* at the Spectacular.'

CHAPTER TWO

Something shifted in the pit of Cos's stomach. It was as if this man thought she and her friends were *things* rather than people – and useless things at that.

Frowning, Miss Meriton held up an envelope. 'But we received our tickets in the post . . .'

Cos knew the handwriting on the envelope well. It was the reason they were here. Her father, Edmund, had just got a job at the Spectacular as a costumier, mending and altering the elegant outfits the dancers and performers needed every day. He'd somehow managed to wrangle Cos and her friends some tickets as a treat.

The man snorted. 'I don't think so, miss. The normal-looking ones are welcome, and, if your more . . . *unusual* charges could step aside, we can let legitimate visitors in.'

Cos immediately knew what this meant. Some of the girls at the Home, like Mary and Pearl, had invisible disabilities, whilst others, such as Diya, who used a wheelchair, had conditions that were far more noticeable. Cos walked the line between the two: on days when her pain wasn't so bad, she was invisible, but as soon as she used her walking stick or needed joint supports, her disability became apparent.

Miss Meriton's cheeks turned crimson. 'You cannot deny some of us entry for no reason. This is a public event! This is . . . discrimination.'

There was an angry whispered discussion between the matron and the attendant before Miss Meriton steered the girls out of the queue, clutching the envelope that had been posted through their door a few days before. 'Girls, I'm going to sort out this misunderstanding. I want you to wait here until I return.' She followed the attendant through the barriers and into the fair, where their fraught discussion continued.

'I *knew* this was an awful idea,' Diya grumbled. 'It always is.'

'Oh, don't say that,' Miles retorted, a grin spreading across his face. 'I'd say the trip to the zoo was an unqualified success. And the circus? Utterly amazing.' He winked at Cos, and she raised an inquisitive eyebrow back at him.

Miles was a new-ish presence in the girls' lives. He was an erstwhile ethical thief and a magnificent street magician who had become firm friends with Cos after he had formed an integral part of their heist at the Treasure Palace. When Miss Meriton became matron, Miles was swiftly hired as the Home's apprentice handyman. Since the Spectacular had appeared in Earl's Court, Miles had feverishly been practising his many tricks in case he got the chance to impress the world-famous magician, the Amazing Luminaire.

Mary let out a horrified shriek, sounding not unlike a kettle on the boil. Cos could just imagine steam funnelling out of her ears. 'I've written reports on both incidents, Miles, and my findings conclude that neither were our fault. They were just unfortunate occurrences in which we *happened* to be present. Really, the clown should have thanked Diya for her quick thinking in putting out the flames.'

'It *was* an excellent opportunity to test how effective my Heartily Helpful Hose was,' Diya conceded.

'And the escaped orangutan at the zoo?'

Miles's question hung heavy in the drizzly evening air. Mary spluttered indignantly as she searched for an answer.

'He looked sad,' Dolly chimed in solemnly. Dolly was one of the younger girls who lived at the Home, and she was fascinated by the wonders of the natural world. 'Orangutans are wild animals; they ought not to be kept in cages – Miss Meriton taught us that in Geography. Besides –' she shrugged – 'I thought he looked rather fetching running around Regent's Park.'

The gaggle of girls erupted into a whirlwind of noise and movement as everyone had their say on the shenanigans of their previous excursions. But thoughts swirled in Cos's head, and she felt her attention wander.

Cos was as excited to visit the Spectacular as her friends, mainly because it gave her a rare opportunity to see her father outside visitors' days. Miss Meriton was far more generous than the Stains had been in allowing the girls to see their families, but for Cos it was never enough – especially when she had twelve years of Dad time to make up for. Like some of the other girls at the Home, Cos harboured the deep desire that she and her father could one day live together like an ordinary family – and, in fact, this was one of the very first questions Edmund had asked her when they'd met. Edmund Deans had swept into Cos's life in a whirlwind of hugs just before Christmas, with unruly brown hair and cheek dimples that matched hers – and the offer of a home for just the two of them, as soon as he got back on his feet.

Miss Meriton had gently explained to him that Cos, like all of the girls at the Home, had conditions that the authorities thought warranted her being raised in an institution. Edmund had thought this over quietly as Cos's heart thundered. *Would he decide that a disabled girl he couldn't raise wasn't worth it? Would he disappear from her life as quickly as he had appeared? Would she become an unwanted burden on him?*

But Edmund seemed to sense Cos's worry, and smiled reassuringly at her as he opened a brass locket that hung from a chain round his neck. Inside was a tiny ferrotype photo, no bigger than the tip of Cos's pinkie finger. Cos gasped: it was a picture of her mother. Willamina Fitzroy smiled at the camera, one eyebrow raised inquisitively. She was dressed scandalously (brilliantly, in Cos's opinion), in a voluminous pair of knickerbockers and matching jacket, and had a star clip pinned in her copper hair.

'You are as bright as a star, just like your mother,' Edmund said gently. 'She named you well.'

Cos blushed. 'You didn't help choose my name?'

Edmund smiled at her. 'I didn't even know Mina and I were expecting a baby,' he admitted ruefully. 'I was banned from seeing her, you see, and as her condition worsened it became far more difficult for her to sneak out. When I found out she had died . . .' His voice cracked and faltered. 'I had no money, but I wanted to do something, *anything*, to pay tribute to her. I stole a bunch of flowers to place on her grave. I was caught, of course. I've been in and out of prison ever since. Only got released for good a year ago.'

Cos swallowed. So Mina had done it all alone – found out she was pregnant, given birth and died, leaving Cos to the mercy of her uncle, Lord Fitzroy, with her name and a badly embroidered handkerchief the only clue to her parentage.

Edmund clicked the locket closed, patting his collar bone where it sat. 'I should've known that Mina would choose such an unusual name: she loved the night sky. She had this saying, you see, one she told herself whenever times got tough. *Keep your feet on the ground, but always remember to look to the stars.*'

Cos felt as though a galaxy of constellations were twinkling inside her heart, bringing light to the darkness that had hollowed her out before. Then and there, she adopted the saying as *her* personal maxim. A golden thread that tied her, through time, to Mina.

Unconsciously, Cos reached towards the old handkerchief that she still kept tied round her neck. It was little more than a tangle of embroidery thread and ripped silk now, but she couldn't bear to take it off.

Edmund frowned. 'What's that?'

Cos sucked in a deep breath. 'My mum made this for me. It was the one item I arrived at the Home with as a baby. I think it was her handkerchief – her initials had been embroidered into the corner. But then she had messily sewed a map on to the silk, with landmarks for me to work out: a heart, bars from a prison cell, a star and X marking the spot.'

'A treasure map,' Edmund breathed.

'A treasure map leading me to you and her. But then Fitzroy got his hands on it,' Cos muttered bitterly, her fingers tangling in the knot of threads.

'I can fix it,' Edmund said with a smile. 'It won't be as good as new, but I can stitch it back together. Mina was never any good at keeping her embroidery neat, but making is my trade.'

Of course, Cos thought. She thought back to the beautifully embroidered love notes that she and Miles had found in Mina's old bedroom. That's how her parents had met: Mina was part of a society for prison reformation and Edmund was a former prisoner, an apprentice tailor who'd gone to prison after stealing food to feed his family.

As if to demonstrate his skills, Edmund dug his free hand into the pocket of his threadbare coat, drawing out a small brass box shaped like a crescent moon. It was dented in places, its colour dulled, but when Edmund turned it upside down Cos gaped. There, engraved upon the bottom of the case, was a message:

MOON,

WHILST WE ARE PARTED, JUST LOOK UP. WE ARE UNDER THE SAME STARRY SKY.

YOURS FOREVER AND ALWAYS,

STAR

Cos found herself grinning.

'This is the final gift Mina gave me,' Edmund muttered softly. He flipped the box back over and unclasped it to reveal

29

a neat row of needles, a pair of scissors, a thimble and spools of thread.

'A sewing kit!' The words burst excitedly from Pearl. In all the excitement of her father arriving for his first visitors' day, Cos had forgotten that the entrance foyer was filled with her friends and their families. 'What a beautiful case – it's probably one of a kind.'

Cos stared. It usually took Pearl a long while to warm to new people, but the thrill of meeting someone who created – like her – seemed to instantly endear Edmund to her.

Edmund smiled sadly. 'The last time we were able to meet, I told Mina I dreamed of starting my own garment-making business. This arrived in the post a while later. When I was finally released from prison, I did it. If you'd let me, I'd love to mend that handkerchief for you, Cosima.'

So Cos untangled her handkerchief and handed it over to Edmund.

He returned it a few weeks later, carefully stitched back together. And now he was working here, at the Spectacular. Cos could have burst with pride.

She came back to the present as she heard Miss Meriton snap in frustration, from inside the Spectacular, 'This is ridiculous. We have the right to visit this attraction just like everyone else.'

A sudden anger fizzed within Cos. Even now, after stopping Fitzroy and his dastardly plan *and* having a kind, clever matron who actually seemed to care for them, Cos was disappointed, but not surprised, to realise that the world at large had stayed the same. Disabled children were still treated differently.

She wasn't going to stand for it any more.

She narrowed her eyes, glaring at the bright lights and twinkling wonders of the Spectacular. On the other side of the turnstiles, rides whirred, jaunty music blared, and the delicious smell of freshly baked cake wafted towards her from the food stalls. Under her breath, she muttered: 'Keep your feet on the ground, but always remember to look to the stars.'

Cos looked around. Instead of fences, rows of fairground wagons marked the boundary between the Spectacular and ordinary London. Each was painted a glossy maroon, embellished with intricate gold stars. Emblazoned across the back of each vehicle in swirling calligraphy was *THE SPECTACULAR*. And tucked away from the grand entrance and its row of turnstiles was a wheelchair-sized space between two of the closest fairground carriages.

Aha, Cos thought. She grinned and turned back to her friends.

'No!' blurted out Diya, before Cos could even open her mouth.

'I haven't said anything yet.'

'I saw that spark in your eyes,' muttered Diya. 'The one that always means chaos.'

Cos barely resisted the urge to roll her eyes. 'Who wants to visit the Spectacular?' she asked the group.

Pearl's hand jolted towards the star-studded London sky. Almost every other girl did the same.

'Why should we visit somewhere that doesn't want us?' Dolly muttered, kicking a crumpled-up Spectacular map into a puddle.

Cos swallowed away the same feeling she was sure Dolly had – one of rejection, again and again. It stung deep in her chest. 'To get even,' she replied defiantly. 'We break in, see the sights, abscond with some yummy treats and head back home. If the Spectacular wants to exclude us, then it deserves to lose the money we would have spent if it had let us in like everyone else.' Cos paused, her heart thumping with an anticipation she hadn't felt in a long while. 'So, who wants to be part of a classic distraction scheme? *With*,' she emphasised, 'a promise of cake if we pull this off.'

Nineteen arms, walking sticks, ear trumpets and other aids waved skywards.

'We *have* to actually get some cake, Cos,' Dolly demanded.

'*In fact,*' signed a girl named Ida, '*we ought to get two cakes each, since we missed out last time.*'

32

That observation was met with nods and murmurs of agreement from the other girls.

'Deal,' said Cos, then turned to her friends, who were in various stages of disappointment, panic and resignation.

'Mary, I'm going to need your planning foresight. I know this is off the cuff, but any bright ideas to help us not get caught would be wonderful.' Cos began to pace back and forth like a general, ignoring the spiky pain in her knees. Like many of her friends' conditions, Cos's disability didn't have an official name, but she dealt with chronic pain and dislocations in all of her joints, and often used a walking stick to help her get around. 'And we *have* to stop by one of the food stalls for cake reasons.'

Mary wiped beads of sweat off her forehead and began to frantically scribble.

'Miles, we might come across some locked doors. Can we count on you?'

In response, Miles twizzled his lock-picking kit between his fingers.

'Pearly, I don't want you to do anything except enjoy seeing that painting.'

The wide grin Pearl gave Cos was as brilliant as every twinkling star in the night sky.

Cos sucked in a nervous breath as she turned to Diya, who seemed just as unimpressed as before. Her mouth was a grim

33

line, her eyes were narrowed and her forehead wrinkled in anger. 'Diya, we can't do this without you and your marvellous inventions. You are the lynchpin in our mechanism.'

Cos thought she saw Diya's disapproval crack a little. Now she just had to nail her down. Cos wore her most innocent expression. 'And didn't you say you were desperate to see the spectacular technological innovations inside?'

'The fairground alone contains all sorts of new inventions,' conceded Diya. Her disapproval melted away as she thought it over, replaced by a kind of wonder. 'It might give me the inspiration to perfect my silent fireworks. All right, I'm in.'

'What do you want the rest of us to do?' called Dolly.

Cos glanced quickly over her shoulder, but Miss Meriton and the attendant's argument seemed to be rumbling on. She gathered the girls closer.

'Here's the plan . . .'

CHAPTER THREE

'Now!' Cos whispered.

The other girls piled towards the orderly queue, dipped under the metal barriers and surged into the Spectacular. The horrified ticket attendant turned away from his argument with Miss Meriton to watch helplessly as the interlopers disappeared into the crowd.

With everyone's attention firmly focused on the girls' – in Cos's opinion – *excellent* distraction, she nodded at Miles, who darted towards the gap Cos had noticed. He was swiftly followed by Mary, Pearl and Diya. Cos grimaced, pausing to quickly rub her aching knee, before hurrying after her friends.

They made it through the gap easily, but before they could slip into the Spectacular Miles suddenly halted, a finger hovering over his lips. They froze as the door of the wagon to their right opened then slammed shut. Cos peered round the corner of the wagon and saw an unassuming lady, her hands covered by a smart fur muff, marching down the steps and darting into the Spectacular.

Cos watched the lady melt into the crowd as Mary also peered round the side of the carriage. 'Wagons for living in, transporting equipment and an office,' she listed, nodding towards the wagon the lady had just left, on which there hung a smart brass plaque reading *THE SPECTACULAR: OFFICE & ENQUIRIES*. 'The map they handed out in the queue is understandably blank about the staff-only sections of the Spectacular.' Mary's fingers vibrated with nerves as she scribbled down these additions to the layout.

'Come on,' Cos muttered, as she tiptoed round the corner of the wagon, before coming to a squelching stop, her friends bumping into her back.

The other girls had scattered into the Spectacular with speed and gusto, their pastel Home uniforms immediately distinguishable amongst all of the grey, navy and black of the other visitors. Hurrying after the girls were a few fairground employees, dressed in the signature red-and-gold uniforms, led by the furious ticket attendant and a rather flustered-looking Miss Meriton.

Cos swore under her breath. They needed to hide – fast.

If they stepped any further into the Spectacular, they'd be spotted straight away.

Mary nudged Cos, nodding back towards the office wagon. 'Let's hide in there whilst we plan our next steps. Miles?'

Miles twizzled open his lock-picking kit and began jimmying the door. As he did so, Diya was already hoisting what looked like a flat metal sheet, lined with grooves, out of the bag attached to her wheelchair.

Cos frowned. 'What's that?'

Diya removed some hooks and shook her contraption. With a *whoosh* it expanded, revealing five more sheets that created a metal slide, slightly wider than Diya's wheelchair and twice as long as Diya herself. As the wagon door clicked and swung open, Diya placed her invention on the stairs, creating a bridge from ground to door.

'I call this my Rambunctious Ramp,' she said, a hint of pride in her voice. 'It's an invention that helps wheelchair users and people with mobility aids get into inaccessible buildings. It should make stairs easier for you, Cos. I made it out of copper offcuts left behind by the builders.'

The builders in question had only just left the Star Diamond Home. The old building hadn't had a penny spent on it in years and was in need of a lot of work to make it accessible to its twenty disabled residents. It had taken months and a whole lot of money to fix, swallowing much of the girls' stolen fortune.

'It's perfect, Diya,' Cos breathed, as always, blown away by Diya's extraordinary ability to transform bits and bobs into useful contraptions. 'After you.'

As Miles ducked into the wagon, Diya lined up her wheelchair with the ramp, then propelled herself forward.

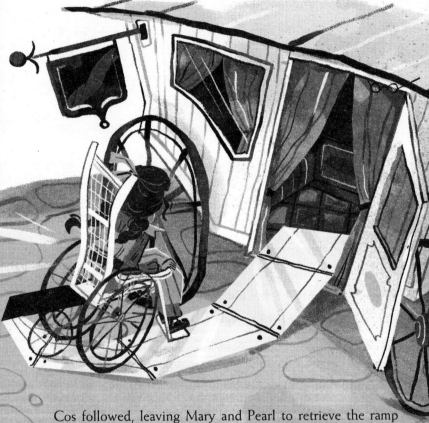

Cos followed, leaving Mary and Pearl to retrieve the ramp before hurrying into the wagon, closing the door gently behind them. They found themselves in a cramped, musty-smelling space containing a small desk and chair. The walls were lined from floor to ceiling with bookshelves, which were stuffed with ledgers and folders and messy bundles of paper, and a small wood-burning stove.

Cos perched on the chair, grateful for the rest sitting gave her knees. Her eyes swept across the desk – crowded with pens and papers covered in messy, almost illegible handwriting. The only words Cos could decipher were 'transfer' and 'controlling shares' – unfathomable concepts that meant nothing to her. But what struck Cos as far more interesting was a worn toy propped up against a lamp. It was a fox, Cos realised.

'Hmm,' Pearl said, smiling at the fox. 'That sort of looks like the things *I* make.'

Pearl was right: the fox did look a little like one of her incredible creations, although it was very old. A button eye was hanging by a thread, and its fur – which Cos supposed had once been a rich russet shade – had faded to a drab muddy colour. But the most unexpected thing about the fox was what it was made of: old sea-lashed rope. Cos would recognise it anywhere: her palms still bore the welts from the years the Stains had forced her to pick apart oakum. Cos's heart raced as she reached out to touch the toy, just to make sure. The child this fox belonged to must have grown up in a similar Home to hers.

Mary peered through the lace curtains, keeping an eye on their seekers. 'I think I can modify our route to the Picture Palace, and we could use some amusement rides as cover so we're not spotted.'

'Aha!' Pearl was rummaging through a crate full of different kinds of material that had been haphazardly shoved by the wood-burning stove. 'These must be old costumes.' She plunged her hand into her pinny and pulled out a needle and thread. 'I think I can disguise our uniforms.'

A few minutes later, Pearl finished inking a rather impressive moustache on Miles's face with a flourish. Cos had a feather boa slung round her neck and wore a velvet jacket. Diya shimmered with sequins, and Mary now wore a hastily pinned silk dress over her Home uniform. They were, in short, a little less recognisable.

Checking that the coast was clear, and utilising Diya's remarkable Rambunctious Ramp for the second time that day, the group crept from the fairground wagon, with Miles carefully locking the door behind them.

Mary darted ahead, her nose buried in her map. Cos and her walking stick squelched after her, followed by Pearl and Miles, who were helping Diya navigate the mud in her wheelchair. Cos scanned their surroundings. She couldn't see any of the other girls or the angry ticket attendant.

Mary tugged on Cos's sleeve. 'This way. The Picture Palace is right beside the Theatre of Illusions, where the performers are. We can use the tent as cover.' She looked around anxiously. 'Wait, where's Miles?'

Whilst Mary liked to plan, Miles was spontaneous. Spotting an opportunity, he had sauntered up to a nearby food stall and was performing a trick for the stallholder whilst secreting cake after cake in his many-pocketed coat. At the conclusion of the magic trick, Miles clicked his fingers. A puff of smoke exploded in front of him. By the time the smoke cleared, Miles had vanished from the stallholder's sight. He appeared back at Cos's side, a little out of breath but with a dimple-making smile wide on his face.

'Cakes secured,' he said with a wink.

Following Mary, they made for the Theatre of Illusions: a sumptuous velvet tent, full of pink-cheeked visitors dressed in their very best: jewels adorned throats, and cufflinks glinted in the twilight. Cos touched a hand to her own precious gem: the glittering star that was always clipped into her otherwise tangled hair, a keepsake that had once belonged to her mother. They weaved away from the crowd, making their way round the curve of the tent, following Mary into the shadows of the evening. Sensibly, Diya switched on a Luminous Lantern to light their way.

A nudge from Pearl snapped Cos out of her thoughts. 'Your

41

dad is somewhere back here, Cos,' she said, nodding towards the tent.

Cos's stomach did a flip that could rival the acrobats'. Cos knew that Edmund's wages at the Spectacular barely covered his rent on a dilapidated room in a boarding house, but it was honest work. She just wished that she could do something to help – not that he would take it. And to be honest, she didn't have much to give. Miss Meriton's wages, proper medical care for the girls and, of course, all the improvements that had to be made to the Home had drained most of the proceeds of the Treasure Palace Heist. Miss Meriton was determined that they fundraise the proper way this time – by attracting aristocratic patronage or asking for donations. Cos knew that it was a much more sensible way to keep the Home going. But, deep down, she missed the thrill that came with outwitting villains and coming up with twisty-turny plans. Her fingers brushed the newspaper in her pocket. If only she were the Spectre, then they'd have enough money to leave all their worries behind . . .

Mary suddenly halted beside another, smaller entrance. The sounds of music and singing drifted towards them. 'A backstage door. Presumably so performers and crew can get some fresh air when they're not on stage.' Mary noted her new discovery on the map. 'Come on, we're almost at the Picture Palace!' She nodded towards a building up ahead.

But Cos peered inside the Theatre of Illusions and immediately froze with wonder. Backstage seemed to be a whirlwind of glittering costumes and people scurrying this way and that . . .

'Cosima?' called a familiar voice.

And, with that, all thoughts of creeping unnoticed to the Picture Palace fell from Cos's mind.

CHAPTER FOUR

os's father stood up from his seat at a small costumier's
table tucked away at the edge of the tent, scattering pins
across the floor. He strode towards her, oblivious to the stares
as he sidestepped dancers and performers, and wrapped Cos
in a hug that pulled her into the theatre tent. Cos breathed
in deeply. In the months since she'd found her father, she'd
learned so much about him.

He always smelled of coffee beans and mint sprigs.

He was never without a needle, spools of thread and his
treasured sewing kit.

The brass locket he
wore on a chain round
his neck now contained
two photos: one of Cos

had joined the older image of Mina.

So much for going unnoticed, Cos thought as Edmund let her go and nodded a hello to her friends, who had joined her in the backstage entrance of the Theatre of Illusions.

'I'm so glad you got the tickets I sent you,' he said, eyes twinkling. There was a gentle murmur through the tent as the rest of the cast and crew went back to their conversations and pre-performance stretches. 'I've been saving my pennies since Christmas so the whole Home could visit!'

Cos hoped her father didn't see her face fall as a wave of shame and regret washed over her. She decided not to mention the incident with the ticket attendant, or the fact that they had technically broken into the Spectacular. She didn't want to do anything to hurt her father, or – even worse – get him in trouble at work.

It was a delicate business, acquiring a father after so many years of not having one. Her father was kind, quiet and gentle, full of hugs and smiles. Cos loved the thoughtful letters he wrote to her every week. He was everything she'd ever wished for, but Cos was brand-new at being a daughter. She didn't know what she was doing and, if she were honest with herself, she was absolutely terrified of messing everything up. Cos was usually phenomenal at talking (sometimes Miss Meriton thought she was a little *too* good), but when she saw her father Cos's tongue got tangled. She stuttered, and her sentences trailed off, and sometimes she silently stared into space as she desperately searched for the right thing to say.

And as she was thinking all this in the gloom of the Theatre of Illusions tent she realised she was doing it again.

'Why are you here? Backstage at the Theatre of Illusions, I mean,' Edmund said, his brows furrowing as he took in their mismatched half-costumed appearance. 'And what on earth are you wearing?'

As Cos scrambled for an answer, Miles helpfully replied for her. 'We're heading to the Picture Palace, so that Pearl can see the famous painting on display. And,' he added, smudging his moustache into a grubby cloud, 'we thought we'd dress for the occasion.'

'Ah – *The Lady Invalid*,' Edmund replied. 'It's a beautiful piece of—'

'DEANS!'

A group of people stood at the other side of the tent. Cos noticed that they had been given a wide berth by everyone else – as if they were different, or separate somehow. Curling round the figures' feet was what Cos could only describe as part cat, part furry beast, a bell jingling on its collar. In fact, it looked almost wild, with a snub nose and long, unruly fur that stuck out in all directions, matted with tangles.

One of the people was a muscular man who wore a skin-tight leotard, striped crimson and gold: the signature colours of the Spectacular. He had swooping hair and a white-toothed grin, and was curling a huge dumbbell up towards his chest. Cos thought back to the advert for the Spectacular she had seen in the *Gazette*. She was sure this must be the strongman: Gustav the Mighty.

Next to Gustav stood the lady who had shouted her father's name. A tiny, bird-like older woman, she was almost swamped by the sumptuous fur coat that was wrapped around her bony frame. She impatiently clicked her fingers at Edmund, and Cos noticed with a shiver that her nails were sharpened to a point.

'I told you before, Deans,' hissed the woman, plucking an ostentatious hat from her head, 'this needs more feathers. I cannot perform my act without them.'

'If you place it on my costume table, Madame Kaplinsky, I'll get that sorted before curtain up,' Edmund promised.

Madame Kaplinsky harrumphed as Cos's gaze shifted to the performer to her left. He was tall and broad with a shining bald head, a curling moustache and a face like thunder. He was exchanging gritted-teeth words with a drab man pacing this way and that. A diamanté bowtie glinted at his throat, and he wore a red velvet suit. As the cat rubbed up against his shin, he ignored it. It yowled mournfully, its fluffy smoke-coloured tail flicking this way and that.

'The Amazing Luminaire,' breathed Miles reverently.

Oh, thought Cos, *the magician Miles so admires.* He was certainly dressed like a star, but Cos sincerely hoped that his expression was a little less furious when he was on stage.

The drab man talking to the illusionist was (in Cos's opinion) rendered even more boring-looking by his proximity to the sparkling performers. He was dressed in an ill-fitting suit and hunched in on himself, as though he thought he could make himself completely invisible. As the cat approached him, he flinched away from it as if terrified.

'That's Sir Theodore Vincent,' her father muttered, nodding towards the haunted-looking man. 'He's an art dealer and a patron of the Spectacular. They're probably discussing final arrangements for the Midnight Masquerade. I've been doing alterations for costumes for it all week – everything from Queen Elizabeth to Cleopatra. They say half of well-to-do London is coming.' Edmund showed Cos his calloused fingers.

'Deans?' This time it was the Amazing Luminaire who barked at Cos's father. 'My diamanté bow tie is fraying. I need it fixed immediately.'

A final figure stepped out from the shadows, placing a gloved hand upon the magician's shoulder. She was a lady, small and ordinary-looking, with mousy brown hair scraped back into a bun and glasses that sat crookedly on her face. The cat-beast steered clear of her altogether, probably wounded by the lack of attention it was getting. Cos realised, with a start, that it was the woman they'd spotted exiting the office wagon.

She must be working for the illusionist, Cos thought.

'Yes, sir,' replied Edmund. 'I'll get working on that right away. My daughter and her friends just popped in for a visit.' He grinned sheepishly at Cos.

The magician's gaze fell on Cos and her walking stick. Immediately his eyes narrowed, in the same way that the ticket attendant's had when they arrived at the Spectacular.

Goose pimples prickled up Cos's arms as Pearl gave her hand a warning squeeze. It seemed that no one at the Spectacular was particularly disability-friendly. They needed to get out of here, and fast.

'Well, we'd better go,' Cos stuttered. 'We don't want to miss that painting.'

Pulling Pearl behind her, Cos limped out of the tent, followed by the others, and they made their way towards the Picture Palace. Every so often, Cos glanced behind them, hoping that the magician – the Amazing Luminaire – hadn't followed them.

They joined the steady stream of patrons entering the Picture Palace, the swell of noise echoing. The huge glass doors opened on to a marble-floored hall bathed in electric light. Cos's neck cracked painfully as she peered upwards towards the glass ceiling that showed the stars twinkling in the night sky.

Ornate golden frames jostled for space across the black walls of the hall. Within each frame were wonders like Cos had never seen. There was a wisteria-draped cottage in the countryside, puffy white clouds dotting the sky. A steely-eyed woman, wearing a diamond necklace, curls cascading over her shoulders. A knight going to war, sunlight glinting off his armour as his sweetheart bade him farewell. Each painting sparked something different within Cos, and she finally understood why Pearl had been so desperate to visit the gallery.

'It's very curious to have an art gallery in the middle of a funfair,' muttered Mary.

A murmur of gentle conversation echoed through the Picture Palace as visitors perused the art in small groups, pausing at each painting for a minute or two. She and her friends were silent, and Cos noticed that they were probably the youngest people in the entire building. Posted just within the doorway were two guards, dressed in their distinctive Spectacular uniform and keeping a keen eye on every visitor who crossed the threshold. Fear danced in Cos's belly, but the guards didn't bat an eyelid – it seemed as though word of their exploits hadn't travelled to this side of the Spectacular.

Pearl suddenly wriggled free of her friends. The thud of her footsteps echoed round the gallery as she darted towards the far end of the building. Well-heeled guests swivelled to track her, and the others rushed to catch up with her. Cos swore under her breath. They were attracting a lot of unwanted attention, and the odd jog-walk she was doing was putting undue strain on her joints.

Leaning heavily on her walking stick, Cos finally realised where Pearl was so determined to get to. The back of the hall, like the other walls, had a black backdrop. Unlike the other walls, there was only one small painting affixed to it, protected by a glass display case. Beneath this case was a glinting steel safe, with a painting-sized door in its roof. Cos's experience in the Treasure Palace Heist told her that if anyone attempted to break the glass the painting would slide inside the vault and the door would slam shut. Two hulking security guards stood – thin-lipped and arms crossed – at either side of the display glass and, beyond them, a plush red velvet rope separated the painting from spectators. It had even more security than the dazzling jewels Cos and her friends had stolen!

Cos was somewhat underwhelmed by her first glance at the art Pearl was so desperate to see: it was a rather ordinary portrait of a young woman with tired eyes and undone hair lying in bed. It sat in an equally ordinary wooden frame bearing a small gold plaque which read: The Lady Invalid *by Ambrose van Hackenboeck, 1686.*

But as she looked closer Cos realised there was so much more to the painting. Whilst the lady's eyes were tired, there was a bright spark within them. Hooked behind her ear was a splendiferous quill with feathers so long they tickled her neck. Upturned books were scattered across her bedspread, and above her head there was a curious contraption – a sort of pulley system attached to a tray, lifting a cup of tea and a plate of biscuits towards her. Cos caught Diya's eye. Her friend's grin was as dazzling as an Edison light bulb.

Cos felt a curious feeling of space within her chest, as though the whole universe had become just a little bit more wondrous. The mysterious lady might be disabled, but she was still living her life fearlessly. Cos had never seen someone like her presented so beautifully.

The scrape of a pencil told Cos that at her other side Mary was already scribbling down additions to her map. Pearl was similarly quiet, her gaze fixed on the painting. She leaned over the rope barrier and peered so closely at it that Cos worried the guards might tell her off. Her face was all amazement. It was beautiful.

The silence was broken by the distant sound of a ruckus. As they turned towards the entrance to the Picture Palace, guests were being barged out of the way, and angry shouts echoed towards them.

As the crowd parted, Cos saw him.

A scowling man scanned the hall. His forehead was slick with sweat, his smart uniform bunched up and creased.

The ticket attendant.

CHAPTER FIVE

'**F**ound you!'

Behind the man were Miss Meriton and Edmund Deans, their faces concerned. The matron rushed across the hall towards them, enveloping them all in hugs. Cos felt a pang of regret for devising a caper that had caused her to worry so.

Edmund followed, frowning. 'Is everything all right? You rushed off so quickly.'

'Oh, girls – thank goodness,' Miss Meriton said with a sigh. 'That's the last of you found.'

'They are intruders – *criminals*,' spat the ticket attendant as soon as Mary had finished explaining. 'They should be being arrested, not comforted.'

'This man is half right, girls,' Miss Meriton said, eyes dark with disappointment now she was satisfied her charges were safe. 'None of you should have sneaked away like that. It was . . . irresponsible. You could have put yourselves in danger. I expect more from you.'

Somehow a telling-off from Miss Meriton was a thousand times worse than any of the horribly cruel punishments the Stains used to dish out. Guilt wormed its way into Cos's stomach, writhing uncomfortably as if she'd eaten one cake too many.

'Having said that,' the matron said, turning back to the ticket attendant, standing up straight and dusting off her skirt, 'the girls only wanted to see the Spectacular, sir. It is an attraction that has been presented as the must-see event in London, that someone in your employ sent us tickets for, and one that you have callously denied them entry to. Can you really blame them for that?'

'My daughter and her friends were denied entry?' Edmund frowned at the ticket attendant. 'For what reason?'

The man drew himself up tall, waving a dismissive hand towards Cos and her friends. 'All employees have been told not to allow people like them in, on the orders of management. They are defectives; they have no place here. This is a fantasy, a place for people to forget their worries for an evening of enchantment. These *children* spoil that illusion.'

As the man's words echoed round the Picture Palace, Mr Gideon Luminaire himself entered the building. Away from the gloom of the theatre, Cos could see that the magician was an unnatural shade of orange, which she assumed was a thick layer of stage make-up. There was a chorus of 'oohs' and a spontaneous round of applause broke out amongst the patrons as his shining shoes squeaked across the gallery floor. Mr Luminaire cracked an insincere smile, his teeth unnaturally white, waving away the attention as though it were an irritating fly.

He was followed by the huge cat, which slunk into the hall, its bell tinkling, and his mousy secretary, who wore a pair of gloves inside.

The Amazing Luminaire paused in the centre of the hall and cleared his throat theatrically. 'Honoured guests, I apologise profusely for the disruption to your visit today,' he boomed. 'Unfortunately, we are going to have to close the Picture Palace momentarily, so please head to one of the Spectacular's many food stalls where my staff will be happy to provide you all with complimentary tea and cakes. If you return in fifteen minutes, you'll find the gallery reopened.'

He looked directly at Cos, Miss Meriton, Edmund, the other children and the ticket attendant. 'But you all stay until we get to the bottom of this matter.'

There was a curious murmur as guests headed towards the glass doors and the promise of free cake. As they did, Mr Luminaire paced back and forth, pinching the bridge of his nose and scowling at the girls. 'Security, leave us,' he ordered, his hand fluttering to his forehead as though he were about to dramatically faint. Cos wondered whether everything the magician did was a performance – every move seemed to be calculated and for show. 'I'm sure you have far more important business to attend to.'

Bowing their heads, the security guards filed out of the building. As Mr Luminaire brought his hand back to his waist, a deck of cards fell from his sleeve, scattering over the floor. Cos and Miles exchanged an eyebrows-raised look – surely a magician of that calibre should know better than to expose a hiding place for his tricks.

The impresario balled his hands into fists and stamped his foot, in a way that reminded Cos of the tantrums younger girls sometimes pitched in the Home.

'Clear this up,' he hissed to his secretary, who nodded, trembling, and began to collect the dropped deck. 'And I assume you have failed to arrange the dry cleaning of my spare costume.' He pulled at his velvet waistcoat. 'Do I have to do everything myself?'

Mr Luminaire and his cat strode towards the children. The cat's fur was dotted with what looked like paint splodges in amber, smoke-grey and inky black. It wore a diamanté collar that looked exceedingly uncomfortable, and its tail flicked as it trotted along.

'I spotted these children in a staff-only area,' Mr Luminaire said, teeth gritted, as he turned to the ticket attendant. 'Why?'

The ticket attendant flinched. 'These degenerate children came into the Spectacular after I refused them entry, sir.'

The Amazing Luminaire's lip curled. 'And why did you do that?'

The ticket attendant seemed momentarily lost for words. 'Well, er, it was, erm . . .' he spluttered quietly, his explanation fading into silence.

Beside Cos, Pearl leaned forward, reaching out a finger to the cat, which had been weaving in and out of Mr Luminaire's legs. The cat hesitated for a moment before booping its nose against Pearl's finger.

The magician opened his mouth again, but before he could say another word there was a tap on his shoulder. He swung round, his coat-tails flapping. 'Yes, Miss Fox?'

The secretary handed Mr Luminaire back his cards. 'Perhaps, sir, you'd like me to deal with the children.' Her voice was soft, and shook with nerves. Cos couldn't imagine the impresario was an easy boss to deal with. 'You're due on stage imminently, and I'm sure you have far more important things to be doing than sorting out such an inconsequential issue.'

Mr Luminaire frowned, then nodded. 'You might be right, Miss Fox. I suppose there's a first time for everything,' he added acidly. 'Deans!'

Cos's father jolted to attention.

'My bow tie. Fix it before curtain up.' He clicked his fingers impatiently, summoning Edmund. The two of them swept from the Picture Palace, Cos's father shooting Cos a worried look as he left. As the huge door swung shut behind them, Miss Fox turned towards Cos and her friends, a relieved expression on her face.

'I am so sorry for this awful misunderstanding,' she said sincerely. 'Please forgive Mr Luminaire. He's been on edge since Sir Theodore allowed us to show the Van Hackenboeck painting. It's this horrible Spectre villain, you see.' She paused for a moment and shook off a shiver.

Cos let out a sigh. Of course the Spectre would target the painting. He'd already stolen some of the world's most famous treasures; a priceless piece of art was sure to be next.

'We've put on extra security,' continued the secretary, 'got the latest in anti-theft innovations, even imported an unbreakable strongbox all the way from Switzerland, yet we're all still terribly nervous. Still, there is no excuse for the abominable way you've been treated today.' She turned to the ticket attendant, whose face was white with rage. 'Apologise, please,' she said firmly. 'And then get back to the turnstiles.'

Grimacing, the ticket attendant murmured an apology before he walked away. Cos's jaw dropped. Other than Miss Meriton and Aggie, she'd never seen another adult stand up for them in that way. Appreciation rushed through Cos as she grinned at Miss Fox, who held out her hand for Miss Meriton to shake. 'Miss Fox, secretary to the Amazing Luminaire.'

'Miss Meriton, matron of the Star Diamond Home for Girls, formerly the Home for Unfortunate Girls.'

Miss Fox blinked, her back ramrod-straight.

'And these are my charges,' continued the matron. 'Cosima's father is a costumier at the Theatre of Illusions – it was he who kindly sent us tickets.'

'Ah, the marvellous Mr Deans!' Miss Fox exclaimed, her expression full of admiration. 'Such a talented tailor, and a kind, if quiet, gentleman to boot. The Spectacular is lucky indeed to have him.'

Cos beamed with pride. The other girls and Miles were too busy petting the cat to have noticed Miss Fox's compliments.

Miss Fox smiled. 'I see you've already made Cat's acquaintance.'

Diya arched an eyebrow. 'He's called Cat?' she spluttered.

'*She* is,' replied the secretary. 'She's a Persian, given to Gideon by a Russian count when we were in St Petersburg. He's allergic to cats, so looking after her became my responsibility and, I have to admit, I'm not really a cat person. So she remained Cat.'

Cat let out a *brrrpp*, as though she thoroughly agreed with Miss Fox.

'Now that we've sorted the unpleasantness,' continued Miss Fox, scooping up the cat-beast which began to wriggle in her arms, hissing in disgust at the unwelcome hug, 'I want you all to have an incredible evening here at the Spectacular. Go on every ride, and make sure not to miss the Great Wheel – it truly is a one-of-a-kind experience. And, to say sorry for the unforgivably rude way you've been treated today, I will reserve front-row seats for you for the show at the Theatre of Illusions tonight.'

She smiled warmly as Cos and her friends descended into excited chatter. Cat leaped from the woman's grip and stalked away, bell dinging as she went, to the delight of Pearl. The girls, Miles and Miss Meriton followed the secretary. 'Well, I'd better head back to my duties. But it was lovely meeting all of you.'

She opened the door, and Cos and her friends slipped through it.

CHAPTER SIX

Cos grinned as she followed Miss Meriton and her friends away from the Picture Palace, back towards the lights and excitement of the fairground. The evening had turned into a brilliant success: she'd hugged her father, the horrible ticket attendant had been told off and the next few hours would consist solely of eating sherbet lemons until their tummies ached, whilst being twirled round and round on the many exciting fairground attractions.

The girls flitted between game-filled stalls and incredible rides, their faces flushed with glee. Miss Meriton rushed after them, tying up shoelaces and treating grazed knees. Diya went on the Steam-Powered Galloper three times before spending half an hour deep in conversation with the man who operated it. Gilded gold chariots and fantastical creatures decorated

Pearl's arms, and many patrons shot the artist admiring glances. Mary quickly decided she did not like rides, and instead looked after hats, pinnies and any other possessions whilst frantically scribbling all over her map, noting down sections and shortcuts not officially recorded.

Cos was captivated by the Great Wheel. It rose so high into the sky, it almost disappeared into the stars. Cos gathered her friends – she almost had to drag Diya away from her chat with the engineer, and it took a lot of cajoling to persuade Mary to even consider stepping foot in one of the wheel's swinging wooden carriages ('Think how much of London you'll be able to map, M!' Cos had promised). But soon she had managed to wrangle Pearl, Miles and Miss Meriton as well, and, using the excellently helpful Rambunctious Ramp, they boarded the platform where each of the carriages docked for guests to embark and alight.

The first carriage that moored at the platform differed from all the others – its glass panels were painted an inky black and studded with stars, blocking their view inside.

'Sorry, loves, that one's broken,' muttered the ride operator as it soared away. Unusually, this Spectacular employee wore a black velvet cloak that hid their face. 'The next carriage will be along momentarily.'

Beside Cos, Miss Meriton jumped, and Cos wondered if she was as scared of heights as Mary. Before Diya had the

63

chance to pepper the operator with questions about the engineering of the Great Wheel, they'd swept away without another word, cloak billowing behind them.

They got into the next carriage without the operator's assistance. The carriage swung as they clambered inside. Even the carriage floor was a large glass panel, and nerves suddenly seemed to shoot through Cos's friends. Mary crumpled into a seat with a defeated moan. Miles scattered his entire deck of playing cards across the floor. Pearl rubbed her arms, blurring her beautiful ink paintings. And Diya seemed to momentarily forget that the wheel was an impressive feat of engineering, and instead screwed her eyes tightly shut.

But feeling unsteady was something Cos was used to. She leaned into the wobbles as their carriage began to lurch upwards. As the wheel revolved higher, the others' unease lessened slightly. Cos and Miss Meriton stood at the very front of the carriage, as if it were a prow on a great ship, staring down as the people, the other rides and even the Theatre of Illusions and the Picture Palace grew more and more distant.

'There's Dolly,' Cos exclaimed excitedly. 'And the other girls. They're all on the spinning teacups again.'

Their carriage lurched higher into the night sky.

'Oh, Pearly, you can really see the stars so much brighter from here. Why don't you paint the constellations?' Miss Meriton asked.

Pearl shuffled gingerly towards the matron and unhooked her paintbrush from behind her ear. Soon Orion and the Great Bear glittered in silver on her arm.

They jolted up again.

'You can see for *miles* from this height – you can see all of London!' Cos added. 'Look – there's the Home, only a few streets away!' She could just about see the crooked tiles of their rooftop, pockmarked with scorches from the Diya–Miles silent firework venture.

With a series of panicked squeaks, Mary tiptoed across the glass floor, unfurling her already transformed map. She began to extend it even further, sketching the tangle of roads that surrounded Earl's Court.

Cos realised that Diya was studiously examining the gigantic axle that rotated the spokes of the wheel. And Miles, after recovering his deck of cards, had also recovered his cheery disposition. He stood beside Cos, pointing out the various landmarks he'd spotted, the only sign of his nervousness his white-knuckled grip on the metal rail.

After what seemed like forever, their carriage reached the summit of the wheel's revolution. London stretched out beneath them, a toy town of buildings and streets. Plumes of smoke melted into the night sky.

'Wow,' whispered Mary.

Cos thought the same. Nothing else needed to be said.

The rest of the ride passed in a contented silence.

They disembarked, passing the cloaked operator again, who turned from them to let the next visitors board the wheel. Then they found the other girls before hurrying over to the last show of the night at the Theatre of Illusions.

Slipping through the velvet curtains into the tent, Cos gasped. Far above her head billowed an ink-black canvas dotted with golden stars – the night sky brought inside. Stomach-churningly tall rope ladders bordered the circular stage, which was painted ruby red. At the rear of the stage, pleated red curtains were drawn. Ringing the stage were rows of plush seats, split by a central passage lit by shimmering floor chandeliers.

'Cos,' groaned Mary, nudging her. 'Keep going. We're holding up the queue.'

Cos stumbled forward, leaning heavily on her walking stick as she picked her way past the crowd, who muttered excitedly as they settled into their seats. The front row had indeed been reserved for them: small cards covered in squiggly handwriting had been pinned to twenty of the best seats, just behind a gaggle of seated musicians, all ready to play their instruments. As they sat down, the lights seemed to be extinguished in a single second, drenching the theatre in darkness. Cos sucked in a deep breath.

A spotlight, suspended from the very top of the tent,

flickered on with a whir, momentarily dazzling Cos. It illuminated a shadowy figure, standing on a podium in the centre of the stage, sporting what appeared to be a rather impressive pair of horns.

All of a sudden, a crackling voice boomed through the tent. 'LADIES AND GENTLEMEN, BOYS AND GIRLS.' *Girls, girls, girls, girls,* echoed around. Beside her, Cos noticed Pearl silently slide her ear defenders over her ears.

'WE ARE DELIGHTED TO WELCOME YOU TO THE THEATRE OF ILLUSIONS.' *Illusions, illusions, illusions, illusions,* whispered back at Cos, sending goose pimples speeding up her arms.

A drum roll reverberated round the tent, and all of a sudden a fanfare burst out.

As Cos's eyes adjusted to the brightness, she recognised the strangely attired figure: it was Gustav the Mighty, the Spectacular's famous strongman. And they weren't horns that protruded from either side of his head, but a long metal bar balanced between his teeth, colossal weights at each end. Cos joined the rest of the audience in a collective gasp. From her front-row seat, she could see the sweat beading on Gustav's forehead, and the way his body shook.

'That should be impossible,' whispered Mary as Gustav unhooked the bar from his jaw and raised it above his head with an almighty roar. 'Nobody's *that* strong.'

She might have said more, but Cos couldn't hear her over the rapturous applause. Gustav's act only became more incredible: he broke slates in half with his bare hands, brought out a troupe of tumbling acrobats and balanced all of them on the tip of his pinkie finger, and bent an iron bar using his thighs.

As Gustav was cheered off the stage, he was replaced by even more wonder: trapeze artists who clambered up rope ladders and spun on their bars far above the ground, sword dancers who threw razor-sharp daggers over their heads, catching the weapons with a flourish and harlequins who juggled with flaming sticks before finishing their act by swallowing the fire whole. Cos clapped so hard that her palms tingled.

Then Madame Kaplinsky emerged from the velvet curtains at the back of the stage, a large emerald glittering at her throat, her fur coat swishing as she slowly made her way into the spotlight. The band switched from a lively march to a slow, scratchy song that sent shivers up Cos's back as the acrobats carefully placed a crystal ball on the podium. Cos realised that Madame Kaplinsky was a spiritualist. She curled her pointed fingernails round the ball, calling on the Other Side to come through. What followed was a spine-tingling show full of ghostly raps that echoed throughout the tent, impossible levitation (although Diya swore she could see wires lifting Madame Kaplinsky) and a message delivered to a sobbing member of the audience from a dearly departed aunt.

Finally, the Amazing Luminaire strode on stage to a standing ovation.

But the 'tricks' the magician attempted were not nearly as good or as believable as the previous acts. He was hopeless at guessing which card he'd handed out to people in the front row; a rabbit appeared before its cue, and spent most of the time chewing on the illusionist's top hat; and when he 'disappeared' in a puff of smoke, Cos saw Mr Luminaire scurrying towards the stage wings. Miles was disappointed, she could tell.

Cos's joints clicked worryingly as the children made their way home. A night chill had set in, and Earl's Court was emptying – snoring children were carried towards the turnstiles by their parents and couples, arm in arm, laid their heads on each other's shoulders. Ahead of Cos, Dolly failed to stifle a huge yawn. She wasn't the only one. Many of the girls blinked away sleep, and Cos's limbs felt as heavy as the coils of old rope they used to pick. Even so, they were happy, their bellies full of toffee apples and candy floss, and their hearts bursting with the thrill of fairground rides.

Suddenly, Dolly skidded to a halt. 'We've forgotten the most important thing!'

Miss Meriton frowned. 'What?'

Dolly turned to Miles. 'CAKE!' she exclaimed, bottom lip juddering dangerously.

Miles grinned toothily. He opened his satchel wide to reveal a host of pilfered treats, only slightly squashed.

The cheer that went up from the girls of the Star Diamond Home echoed into the night. Cos joined in, whooping loudly. It wasn't until much later, half asleep and tucked up in bed, that she realised she'd left more than her heart behind at the Spectacular.

The precious star clip that had once belonged to her mother, the one she never took off, not even to bathe, was gone.

CHAPTER SEVEN

Visitors' days always sent a frisson of excitement through the Home. The floors were swept, cutlery polished till it shone and the tables in the dining hall set with teapots and cups. Cake stands were filled with the stolen Spectacular pastries, alongside homemade scones, finger sandwiches and petits fours. A beautiful banner, created by Pearl, was strung across the entrance foyer, and a cluster of girls peered out of the library window, anxiously awaiting the arrival of their families. Miss Meriton had even taken a break from her preparations for the Home's upcoming inspection to ensure that the girls' latest work was displayed fetchingly for their visitors' perusal.

Cos tore through the library like a tornado, upending cushions, peering under Mary's maps, which covered the desk, and flicking through heavy tomes in her desperate hunt for her star clip. She had already scoured the dormitory and the kitchen, but as every search ended in nothing her heart sank lower and lower.

'How's it going?' squeaked Mary, as she began to carefully organise the piles that Cos had rifled through.

As soon as Cos had discovered that her star was missing, Mary had offered to coordinate the search. She'd used complicated words like 'methodical' and 'systematic', which Cos didn't understand fully, but it did sound as though they were the most sensible approach to locating her lost treasure. Dread blazed bright in Cos's chest and before she knew it she had tipped over the apple crate by her bed, scattering her possessions. She had continued the hunt for her star all morning, leaving a trail of destruction in her wake.

She ran her fingers through her hair, catching them in the lion-like tangles that always appeared in her mane overnight. 'I've searched everywhere, Mary,' she said, swallowing a sob. The star clip was one of the few items she had that had belonged to her mother, and losing it felt a little bit like discovering she had a mother *and* finding out she was dead all over again. 'I'm beginning to think it really did fall off at the Spectacular, and if it did I have no chance of ever finding it again.'

Mary placed a comforting hand on Cos's back. 'It'll turn up, Cos. I'm sure of it.'

'I still can't find my favourite screwdriver,' muttered Diya with a scowl. 'Seems like lots of things are going missing.'

Cos bit her lip to stop herself from snapping at her friend. She was finding it very difficult to care about a misplaced screwdriver when she'd lost her mother's star. She searched her pinny pocket for what felt like the thousandth time that day, but there was no star clip, only her dog-eared copy of the *Gazette*.

'They're coming! I see them!' yelled Dolly, scattering Cos's thoughts. The small girl skittered towards the entrance foyer, excited to see her mother and father. In an instant, the library exploded into a whirlwind of noise and movement as chattering girls hoisted themselves up with the help of mobility aids to follow Dolly.

'Are you coming?' Mary nudged Cos.

Cos nodded absentmindedly, stepping closer to the window to get a better look at the group striding towards the Home. 'I'll be there in a moment. You go ahead.'

She recognised most of the approaching people: Mary's grandad dressed in his Sunday best, Diya's mother and siblings, and Pearl's formidable Aunt Birdie and her signature many-feathered hat. But there was only one person Cos wanted to see.

Edmund Deans seemed to gleam in the dullness of the March morning. He was attired in his Spectacular finery,

74

embroidered stars dotting his blue velvet suit, but over that he wore his favourite threadbare coat. Draped round his neck was his tape measure and slung across his chest was a kit bag, his costumier's scissors peeking out. He was chatting with Diya's older brother as he walked, an easy smile on his face.

Cos's heart squeezed as she pushed herself away from the window and followed the others. This was actually happening. Cos had yearned to have family visit her at the Home since she could remember, and for a long time it had felt like an impossible dream. Every now and again she would pinch herself, just to double-check that all this was real. She set aside her worry about her missing star clip and pasted a smile on her face.

She stepped into the entrance foyer as Miss Meriton opened the wooden doors, and a breeze whooshed in with the relatives. In a whirl of welcome hugs and hellos, their family members strode inside.

Pausing on the threshold, Cos grinned as she caught her father's eye. He smiled back, ducking past girls and relatives as he swooped Cos into the air before pulling her close. Every hug was just as special as the first one.

'Welcome, everyone,' Miss Meriton said. 'If you'd like to follow me into the dining hall, we will be serving tea and cakes.'

*

Laughter and chatter rumbled across the dining hall as steaming tea was poured into cups, and cakes were devoured. Cos sat at a table with Diya, Mary, Pearl, Miles and their families, her father on her right-hand side. The others were deep in conversation with their visitors, and Pearl's Aunt Birdie was currently casting her discerning eye over her niece's latest artwork at the far side of the hall.

But today silence stretched between Cos and her father. Cos didn't like silence very much. It set her teeth on edge. Miss Meriton insisted that it was perfectly normal and that as they were still getting to know each other, completely understandable. Still, Cos liked to fill the silence as soon as she could.

As she opened her mouth to ask something – anything – there was a tap on her shoulder.

'Cos, darling, we've run out of milk,' Miss Meriton said, her arms full of crumb-smeared plates and used cups and saucers, stacked teeteringly all the way to the matron's chin. 'Do you think you and Mary could pop to the shop to get us some more? I would go myself, but I'm afraid I must start on the washing-up.'

Cos swallowed her question for Edmund and nodded. 'Of course, Miss Meriton.' She and Mary pushed back their chairs. 'We'll be back soon – the shop's only round the corner.'

Mary's grandpa wheezed out a cough that rattled his chest.

'Is that wise?' he rasped, his voice barely more than a whisper. 'Two disabled children out on their own might be dangerous.'

Miss Meriton smiled serenely. 'It's important for the girls to experience the world as they grow older, Mr Anderson, and for the world to experience their marvellousness. Cosima and Mary are more than capable, and I have every faith in them.'

Mary gave her grandpa's hand a squeeze before following Cos and Miss Meriton to the entrance foyer, where the matron handed them a few coins and bade them goodbye.

Mary grinned as she twisted a scarf, knitted by Pearl, round Cos's neck. 'I bet it's windy out there,' she prophesied as she pushed open the front door.

CHAPTER EIGHT

Mary was right. The wind whipped Cos's curls into tangles. 'We can do this,' Mary said, mainly to herself, as she hooked her arm round Cos's and pulled the door shut. 'In order to be brave, you have to face your fears. Shall we count the steps?'

Miss Meriton was an expert on children's disabilities, regularly corresponding with other experts the world over. She had been working with many of the girls to help them thrive with their conditions, not in spite of them.

The matron had presented Cos with an exercise plan that she had designed to help build her strength, lessen the chance of dislocations and ease her persistent gnawing pain. Mary's goal was to spend more time outside the Home. The years the Stains had locked them away from the outside world had made her especially jittery when she left it. Both girls had found that counting the steps to and from their destination helped Mary not to fixate on potential panic whirlwinds, and distracted Cos from her pain.

The corner shop was exactly 537 steps from the Star Diamond Home. They got there without incident, and bought a pint of milk.

Mary let out a trembly breath. 'I did it. And without a panic whirlwind.'

Cos gave her friend's arm a supportive squeeze, but her thoughts had drifted away – a little further up the road from the corner shop, towards Earl's Court.

If I could pop to the Spectacular for just a moment, she thought, *maybe I could find my star clip. That lady – Miss Fox – seemed lovely, and I'm sure she'd help. Perhaps it's been handed in to lost property.*

Mary was tugging at her sleeve. 'Come on, Cos – my grandpa will want another cuppa before he returns to the workhouse. He says the tea there is like dirty dishwater.'

'Can we just check if someone's handed in my star clip at the Spectacular?' Cos pleaded. 'It's only five minutes down the road, and my joints are feeling good. We'll be back before you know it, I promise.'

Mary agreed half-heartedly, and Cos set off with a spring in her step. But as they neared Earl's Court her hope fizzled out. There was something odd about the people outside the

Spectacular. Instead of the usual winding queue, a crowd had gathered.

Soon Cos and Mary were in the crowd, craning their necks to try to see what was going on. Mutters and whispers travelled fast around the gathering. Cos elbowed her way past, with Mary squeaking apologetically to the people they'd displaced.

As she reached the front of the crowd, Cos caught sight of a banner that had been strung above the turnstiles, fluttering wildly in the breeze. It read:

We regret to announce . . .

The unavoidable and unforeseen closure of

THE SPECTACULAR

UNTIL FURTHER NOTICE.

Cos frowned. The Spectacular wasn't due to close till next week. It had been so packed the day before and, by the look of the crowd around them, many visitors had been planning to go today as well. Disappointed sighs and children's sobs surrounded Cos and Mary, who, at the sight of the sudden unfortunate news, had begun to fidget nervously.

Cos pulled her friend away from the crowd, looking to find

them a quieter place whilst Mary counted away her worry. As she slowed her own breaths in an attempt to help ease Mary's whirlwind, her thoughts spun. *What unexpected event had led the Spectacular to close so suddenly?* She thought of her father with a pang. He didn't – *couldn't* – know about this, or he would've said. He was going to be devastated. The Spectacular was his first proper job since he'd been released from prison, and he had pinned all his hopes on it igniting his costuming career. She forgot all about her missing star clip.

Cos spotted a quiet alcove with a bench, away from the turnstiles, for Mary to calm her shaking hands. As they neared the bench, Cos heard a heated debate.

'It can't be closed for any other reason,' said a man with an upturned nose and a head full of buttery curls. A small girl with the same upturned nose, wearing a many-frilled dress, hung from his hand, her face blotchy with tears. 'It's clear. The Spectre has struck again.'

The small girl let out a cry that was not unlike a ship's horn.

The Spectre? Here? In Kensington? Cos tensed. Beside her, Mary let out an anguished groan.

'Pah,' replied a reedy-voiced lady. In her arms she carried a crying baby, who had a single buttery-coloured curl in the centre of his head. 'Don't be so dramatic, Donald. It could be closed for many reasons – the weather, injury, illness.' Her voice dropped to a hiss. 'And refrain from

81

mentioning that thief's name – you'll scare the children.'

Donald huffed indignantly. 'It's obvious, Lavinia. The Spectre was bound to come to England soon enough.' He shrugged, and his curls did too. 'He's been waiting, biding his time.'

'BALDERDASH,' replied Lavinia, her lips pursing. 'You are just gossiping like an old maid. You have no idea why—'

The lady suddenly stopped when she noticed Cos staring. She nudged her husband. Cos tried her best to rearrange her face into an innocent expression. As the family strode away, Cos's mind raced. The Spectre *might* be involved in the mysterious closing of the Spectacular. But what had he stolen?

Cos turned and stared at the curiously empty Spectacular. Its stillness was in stark contrast to the usually bustling event; stalls were boarded up and no workers crisscrossed the central concourse of the gigantic site. Grumbles rose up from the gathered crowd; they were waiting for an event that would never open.

And then, just as Mary muttered a quiet, 'Can we go now, Cos?', a flat-capped boy darted towards the crowd, elbowing his way into its centre. He had a grubby face, a wide smile and a ragged set of clothes, full of patches and holes.

The boy cleared his throat, holding a piece of paper taut to read from it. 'BREAKING NEWS!' he shouted, his voice carrying with the breeze. 'PAINTING STOLEN FROM THE SPECTACULAR.'

The gathering gasped. Cos's heart sank. Mary's bottom lip wobbled dangerously. An eerie hush fell as everyone waited for the newspaper boy to say more.

'SCOTLAND YARD SAY THAT THE VAN HACKENBOECK DISAPPEARED OVERNIGHT. A NE'ER-DO-WELL WITH A CURLED MOUSTACHE, DRESSED IN FINERY AND WEARING A POLKA-DOT NECKTIE, WAS SEEN EXITING THE PREMISES AS POLICE ATTENDED. LEFT AT THE SCENE OF THE CRIME WAS A CALLING CARD WITH THE SPECTRE'S SIGNATURE SCRAWLED ACROSS IT.'

The crowd erupted into a tangle of noise: a buzz of chatter mixed with shouts and gasps. The woman had been right: the Spectre *was* in London.

'DETECTIVES SAY THEY ARE CLOSING IN ON A SUSPECT. VINCENT & SONS, ART DEALERS, OFFER A £250 REWARD FOR THE PAINTING'S SAFE RETURN.'

More chatter. Cos frowned. From everything she'd read about the Spectre – and she'd hungrily devoured every newspaper article on the master thief – one thing had been made clear: police across the world had no idea who the criminal really was. How had Scotland Yard managed to find a prime suspect in just a few hours?

The boy cleared his throat again, his cheeks apple red at the attention his proclamations were attracting. 'FIND OUT

THE FULL STORY, ONLY IN TOMORROW'S *GAZETTE*.' With a doff of his cap, the boy carefully rolled up his poster and darted from the crowd. Cos could hear him calling as he stalked down another street, his shouts of 'BREAKING NEWS' getting fainter and fainter until they faded into the general noise of Kensington.

Mary's tug on her sleeve became even more insistent.

'Let's get home,' Cos muttered, her thoughts spinning.

'STOLEN?' yelled Diya.

The girls and their relatives had burst into a frenzy of chatter as soon as Cos and Mary had announced the news: the Spectacular was closed till further notice, and its prized painting had been stolen by the infamous thief, the Spectre, brazenly clad in expensive clothes and a polka-dot necktie. It had taken a fresh serving of scones and another round of tea for the gossiping to die down.

Cos slumped into her chair, her thoughts jumbling in her head. Her father hadn't said a word since he heard the news. *He must be in shock*, Cos thought. He sat pin-straight at the table, gripping his bag tightly, his expression frozen and his mug of tea going cold. He wouldn't, after all, be going into work tonight. Cos wondered if he was worried about losing much-needed wages. She wished she could do something to help. Having spent so long in prison, crime was a bit of a sore spot to Edmund. It was ironic, really, Cos thought. Edmund had tried desperately to go straight and get some honest work, and a theft might put all that in jeopardy.

Pearl was equally devastated. She shook in her seat, her arms wrapped round herself for comfort.

'It's all right, Pearl,' Cos promised, not at all sure of the truth of her words.

Pearl shook her head defiantly. 'It's not, Cos.'

Cos scrambled for a way to reassure Pearl. 'The newspaper boy said detectives were close to solving the case. And the suspect was a man wearing a distinctive necktie, remember? Maybe the Spectre is finally about to be caught!'

All of a sudden, Cos's dad pushed back his chair and stood up. Cos frowned, but before she could ask him what was wrong there was a short, sharp rap on the front door.

'That's odd,' Miss Meriton said with a frown as she scanned the dining hall. 'All our guests are present and accounted for. Unless . . .' A smile broke across the matron's face. 'Could Aggie have finished her latest investigation?'

The possibility of an Aggie visit even managed to coax a watery smile out of Pearl, and all of the girls, and most of their visitors, piled into the entrance foyer to greet the unexpected guest.

CHAPTER NINE

M iss Meriton pulled open the door. The girls and their families fanned out behind the matron, peering curiously at whoever it was that stood on the doorstep. Cos realised immediately it was not Aggie. *She* usually turned up at the Home with an armful of papers, a mischievous grin on her face as she swept in the door, full of stories about her latest investigative quarry.

Cos barely caught a glimpse of the stranger at the front door – the silver glint of a filigree badge, the shine of polished buttons on a navy coat – before he barrelled into the entrance foyer without introducing himself. Before Miss Meriton could protest, the gentleman drew a small card from his coat pocket and thrust it into the matron's face. It read:

DETECTIVE CONSTABLE

WARRANT CARD

TO WHOM IT MAY CONCERN

This is to certify that the bearer,

John Wensleydale

is a member of the METROPOLITAN POLICE SERVICE,

No. 3 District.

Sir Edward Bradford, Commissioner of Police

'Detective Constable Wensleydale at your service, ma'am,' boomed the man. Miss Meriton gently shut the front door.

A police officer, thought Cos, an icy fear creeping up her throat. *That newspaper boy said that the police were closing in on the suspect. This detective couldn't suspect* them, *could they?* Cos knew that she and her friends were more than capable of such an impossible theft, but on this occasion they were entirely innocent. Besides, the Spectre was an *international* art thief, and Cos and her friends had never left the country.

'Apologies for my abrupt entrance, but I am here on a matter of utmost importance. I'm investigating a theft. Last night, a priceless painting was stolen from the Spectacular.' His beady eyes scanned the foyer. 'I have been informed of a certain . . . *allegation.* Mr Gideon Luminaire told us that your charges broke into the Spectacular yesterday and visited the now-stolen painting. Is this true?'

87

Cos's stomach pitched, as if she'd taken a step into the road and narrowly missed being hit by a carriage. Beside her, Mary whimpered. Pearl looked ashen and Diya began twizzling her second-favourite screwdriver between her fingers – a telltale sign of nerves. Even Miles looked slightly worried.

Cos winced as she heard Pearl's Aunt Birdie exclaim, 'Breaking and entering? Well, I never! I have half a mind to demand my Pearl be removed from this establishment immediately.'

'It wasn't like that!' Cos's words left her mouth before she had a chance to think them through. She rounded on Aunt Birdie, who narrowed her beady eyes at her. 'We just wanted to see the painting like everyone else,' she explained, hating the way her voice came out so mouselike in front of the glaring Detective Constable Wensleydale.

Detective Constable Wensleydale's lip curled, and he plucked his pipe from his mouth. 'This is a home for *unfortunate* children, madam?' he asked Miss Meriton, his gaze flitting towards the girls.

Miss Meriton pursed her lips. 'No, this is the Star Diamond Home for Girls. The girls who live here have a variety of disabilities and conditions. We don't use the word "unfortunate" because—'

'And what is going on here today?' interrupted Detective Constable Wensleydale, waving his pipe towards the gathered children and their families.

'A visitors' day,' explained the matron promptly. 'We have them regularly – a chance for the girls to spend valuable time with family and friends.'

'How *interesting* . . .' muttered the detective incredulously, as though this was a most suspicious occurrence. Cos shifted uncomfortably as he traipsed across the entrance foyer, peering closely at everything, from the floor to the comfy armchair to the many pictures hanging on the walls. 'What is this?' he boomed suddenly, jabbing his pipe towards a watercolour painting that occupied the wall space between the kitchen and Miss Meriton's office.

'Er, that is a painting of my mother,' Miss Meriton said, following the detective over to the portrait. 'It was done by one of my talented charges.' She beamed at Pearl, who blushed and twiddled with the ribbon in her hair.

Wensleydale knitted his eyebrows together in a scowl. 'Not that one, *this* one.' He pointed a stubby finger at an old tintype photograph hanging wonkily next to Pearl's beautiful artwork.

The photo was one of the many historical treasures discovered during the Home's recent renovations. Unbeknownst to Cos, who had always believed that she'd been the first, the building had long been a place where disabled girls spent their childhoods, and when the builders found reams of old photos, toys and records up in the attic, Miss Meriton insisted that everything be kept. 'It's your history,' she had told them reverently, as she wielded a hammer and nail to squeeze the photo into the already crowded wall space of the foyer. 'It's important.'

The tintype was a black-and-white photo of a group of girls, smiling in front of the entrance to the Home. They all wore frilly white pinafores over drab grey dresses and had identically plaited hair. Some sat in wheelchairs, while others leaned on crutches or held ear trumpets. At the bottom of the photo was a neatly written caption: *Home for Unfortunate Girls, 1887.*

'AHA!' exploded the detective, rounding triumphantly on Miss Meriton. 'The first lie. This *is* a home for unfortunates.'

'It wasn't a lie.' Edmund spoke quietly, but his words cut through the air like a knife. 'If you'd let Miss Meriton speak, you would have heard her explain that although some children's homes have old-fashioned names like "unfortunate" and "incurables", here the focus is on all the amazing things the girls can do.' He gave Cos's arm a squeeze.

Wensleydale blinked at Edmund, whose rolled-up sleeves showed off his tattooed tribute to his lost love, Mina: constellations dotted his forearms. He appraised him for a long moment, puffing out a cloud of foul-smelling smoke from his pipe. Then he turned to Miss Meriton. 'As you have already seen, I have a search warrant for the building,' he said.

'To rule you and your charges out conclusively in this matter.'

Cos sucked in a worried breath. *This was . . . absurd.* It seemed as though the detective really believed that the missing painting might be here. Miss Meriton gave the detective the barest of nods. With a final puff on his pipe, Wensleydale disappeared into the belly of the Home.

Room by room, Detective Constable Wensleydale searched the Star Diamond Home. He rummaged through drawers, prised up floorboards and rifled in cupboards. Most of the girls and their families had returned to the dining hall whilst the building was searched, but Cos, her father, Diya, Mary, Pearl and Miles trailed after the policeman, their eyes narrowed in suspicion. Miss Meriton headed their little party, her lips becoming more and more pursed with each carelessly thrown belonging.

Finally, Detective Constable Wensleydale finished his search. He had found nothing. His breaths came out fast and hard, and sweat beaded on his wrinkle-creased forehead. A vein bulged in his neck.

The tightness in Cos's chest eased. She still didn't understand why the detective had been so sure that he would find *The Lady Invalid* in the Home, but she could worry about that later. Right now, Cos just wanted him gone – his tobacco-tinged whiff hung in the air and clogged in her throat.

As she and Diya rode the newly installed lift down to the

ground floor, they could hear Wensleydale clatter down the rickety staircase, muttering bitterly under his breath. The lift dinged open, just as Edmund strode towards the front door to let the policeman out.

At that moment, time seemed to warp and jolt, as though Cos had entered one of those new-fangled moving pictures. As Cos's father reached the door, she noticed something odd poking out of the top of the bag, which was slung across his back – a right angle made out of wood. Wensleydale had noticed it as well, and a triumphant snarl creased his face.

Edmund pulled the door open. A beam of sunlight illuminated a shaft of dancing dust motes. Cos saw that the right angle wasn't just a right angle, but a frame.

Her stomach dropped. Before Cos could find any words, the detective slammed the front door shut, pushed Edmund against it and grabbed the bag from her father's shoulder.

Then, ever so slowly, he plucked out an old, empty picture frame. There was a small brass plaque at the bottom of the frame, with an inscription Cos couldn't quite make out.

Pearl and Mary gasped.

'*The Lady Invalid*,' Pearl muttered.

'The frame of the stolen painting,' whispered Mary breathlessly.

'The Spectre!' growled the policeman, grabbing hold of Edmund's shirt and shaking him roughly. 'Where's the rest of it?'

Edmund shook his head, his expression unreadable.

Wensleydale unhooked a pair of clinking handcuffs from his belt, and slid them on to Edmund's wrists. He looked triumphant. 'You're under arrest.'

Cos was numb with shock, unable to say or do anything. She was vaguely aware of arms around her, and comforting words muttered into her ear. Her father couldn't be the Spectre. It was impossible. The Spectre must have put it in his bag to frame him.

The door was opened again. The strong breeze from outside whirled her thoughts into a tornado.

As he was pushed through the front door, Edmund locked eyes with Cos. 'I didn't do this, Cosima. I promise you!'

CHAPTER TEN

Cos's walking stick clattered to the floor and her legs gave out beneath her. Pain shot through her, but nothing hurt as much as the pain in her heart. *Her dad was gone – no, he had been taken.* Everything was hazy and tear-blurred. She sat on the floor, staring into nothingness, as shoes marched past her, the murmurs of goodbyes echoing through her skull. A blanket was gently tucked around her shoulders, a steaming mug of hot cocoa placed by her feet and her knee support fetched from the medical room.

Mechanically, Cos straightened her leg and pulled on her support, clasping it tightly round her kneecap. Someone helped her to her feet and handed her walking stick to her. She gripped it tightly. She was shaking so much that she could feel her kneecaps rattle, and she leaned heavily on the arms that supported her.

'It'll be all right, Cos,' Miles murmured into her ear. 'We'll figure it out, I promise.'

'They took him away.' A scratchy, whining, not-Cos voice sounded from her throat.

Diya's face sharpened into focus. She was guiding Cos towards the door leading to the entrance foyer. Her expression was a swirl of worry and shock and concern.

'He's not guilty, Diya,' Cos rasped. 'I *know* he didn't do it. They're only arresting him because of his past.' She knew Wensleydale had spotted her father's prison tattoos.

An unwanted thought scurried into Cos's head. And her father had been arrested because of the empty frame of the painting that had been in his bag. It must have been planted on him, Cos decided. Someone wanted him framed. But why?

Before Cos could think on that more, she was gently deposited into a comfy armchair that sat in the corner of the entrance foyer. A blanket was folded on her lap and her walking stick clicked into the holder at the armrest of the chair.

Cos caught the scent of peonies as Miss Meriton hurried into the entrance foyer, grabbing her coat and twirling it on in one movement. Her face – usually unflustered and calm, no matter what situation she was in – was crinkled with worry. The matron knelt before Cos, cupping her face in her palms.

'Cos, I know you must be feeling hopeless. I'm so sorry that you had to be there to see your father arrested. It isn't fair, especially so soon after you found each other. I refuse to lie to you. Finding the stolen painting's missing frame in his possession is pretty damning evidence, and Edmund has a criminal past. I can't say if your father is innocent.'

'He is,' Cos interrupted fiercely. She dug her hands into her pinny pocket, grabbing her jam-stained, crumpled copy of the *London Gazette* and brandishing it at the matron. 'Look – it says here that the Spectre struck in New York just before Christmas, and in Berlin and Paris earlier last year. I'd be surprised if my father's ever left the country. He hasn't got the money, and he's spent most of the past decade in prison.'

'Those are very valid points. The circumstances surrounding his arrest are . . . suspicious,' continued a measured Miss Meriton.

Cos was so used to adults dismissing her out of turn that she was still surprised when Miss Meriton took her thoughts seriously. 'And I know exactly who to contact when potential injustices like this happen . . .'

'Aggie,' breathed Cos, thinking back to their patron's constant determination to right wrongs. She frowned. 'But she's undercover at the moment. Uncontactable.'

Miss Meriton crooked an amused eyebrow. 'Ah, she's

uncontactable to everyone but me. I *always* know her location in case of emergencies. And this is most definitely an emergency.'

Cos blinked as Miss Meriton planted a kiss on her forehead. 'Can we come with you?'

Miss Meriton pursed her lips. 'She's doing an investigation, Cos. If all of us go, we might blow her cover. She's not far from here. I will be back within the hour. Besides, you need rest. Diya, I've gathered the girls into the schoolroom. Most are understandably upset about visitors' day being cut short so abruptly, so I've decided there will be no lessons for the rest of the day.'

Diya deflated – she loved lessons – whilst Pearl visibly brightened. If Cos wasn't in such pain, she might have giggled. Pearl was not a fan of lessons, and much preferred to spend her day crafting, painting and creating freely.

'As you're so delighted about that, Pearl,' said Miss Meriton, the ghost of a smile about her lips, 'I'm sure you'll be happy to help Diya keep an eye on everyone. Make sure everyone has plenty of water, and fetch books and games if they so wish.'

Pearl and Diya nodded.

'Miles,' continued Miss Meriton, business-like, 'I suspect most of the girls will be full of cake for the foreseeable future, but, just in case I am delayed, can you make a start on dinner? It doesn't need to be fancy; sandwiches will do.'

'Of course, miss,' Miles replied.

'Mary, can I trust you to keep on top of medications? I'm not planning to be gone long at all, but you know how fast chronic conditions can change.'

Mary nodded solemnly, flicking quickly to a piece of paper fastened to her clipboard that was titled *MEDICATIONS – TYPES, TIMES + EFFECTS* and sat above a complicated-looking table. Miss Meriton handed her a glinting silver key.

Miss Meriton huffed out a breath, and Cos realised the usually unflappable matron was nervous. Her gaze fell to Cos again, and she reached forward to give her hand a comforting squeeze. 'I'll be right back, and I'll bring Aggie, and together we will work out a way to help Edmund,' she promised. 'Mary – fetch Cos some laudanum, will you? I think the pain might be getting to her.'

Then, with one final swish of her coat, Miss Meriton left. Mary hurried away, returning with a small tablet and a glass of water. Cos swallowed the pain medication, tucked her copy of the *Gazette* into the armchair and surrendered to the fog enveloping her. Her eyelids fluttered closed.

Miss Meriton will come back with Aggie, and then everything will be all right, Cos told herself as she drifted into a dreamless sleep.

Cos woke to starlight pouring in through the bay windows,

casting the entrance foyer in shadows and darkness. She blinked away her sleepiness, hesitantly straightening and bending her leg. The pain had dulled to a constant ache.

For a moment, she was confused. Miss Meriton was usually so strict about not letting girls nap in the entrance foyer. Then the awfulness of the day flooded back – the stolen painting, the empty wooden frame, her father being led away in handcuffs.

Just as sadness threatened to envelop Cos, she noticed that she wasn't alone. Surrounding her armchair were her friends: Pearl, Miles and Diya were all snoring softly, whilst Mary – wide awake – was frantically scribbling on a piece of paper attached to her clipboard.

'Whassatime?' Cos yawned.

'Gone midnight,' Mary whispered back. 'The other girls are all asleep in the dormitory, but you looked so peaceful here, we didn't want to move you. And we didn't want you to wake up on your own.'

Gratitude rushed through Cos. Even when she felt at her absolute worst, she could always count on her friends.

'Wait,' she said, a little louder than she'd intended, her voice echoing in the foyer. She paused for a moment as Diya stirred before falling back to sleep. 'Is Miss Meriton not back with Aggie?'

Mary shook her head, her fingers trembling. Cos

frowned. It was unheard of for Miss Meriton to leave them unsupervised for more than a few minutes, let alone hours.

'I'm sure there's a reasonable explanation,' Mary squeaked. Cos was sure she didn't believe a single word she was saying. 'They'll be back by breakfast – you'll see.'

Doubt crept into Cos's chest. By breakfast it would almost be a whole day since the visitors'-day debacle and Miss Meriton's hurried departure. But, even as those nerves spun round her head, a yawn caught Cos off guard.

Mary cocked her head, doing her best Miss Meriton impression. 'You need sleep, Cos. You've had a very difficult day – both for your joints and your mind. You won't be any use to your father if you're too tired to function.'

She stood up and began to fuss around Cos – smoothing her unruly hair and tucking in her blanket. As Mary leaned in to kiss Cos's forehead, Cos spotted her friend's swollen, grey eyebags – the telltale sign that she was worn out.

'Fine,' Cos said, stifling another yawn. 'But on one condition.'

'Go on,' Mary said warily.

'You put down that clipboard and sleep as well,' Cos demanded. She scooched over, patting the newly free space. 'You can squeeze in with me.'

Mary sighed, but placed her clipboard down and flopped into the chair next to Cos, pulling the blanket over her as well. As Mary's whistling breaths deepened, Cos found herself losing the battle to stay awake.

'Cos! Cos!'

Cos was shaken from her slumber by a number of bright-eyed girls, still dressed in their nightclothes. She blinked at them. Sunlight streamed in through the windows.

'There's someone at the door.'

Cos shot up, ignoring the groan from her joints. She nudged Diya with her walking stick, and shook Mary awake. Miles was already stretching, and Pearl was uncurling from her cat-like snooze.

A shadow was silhouetted in the morning sunshine at the front door. Hope stuttered into Cos's heart. Maybe it was Miss Meriton? Or the detective, coming to admit he had the wrong man? Perhaps, Cos's hopeful heart dared to dream, it was Edmund Deans himself, freshly cleared of all wrongdoing.

She yanked the door open, full of excitement.

On the front step was a woman. She wore a smart brown dress and carried an official-looking clipboard and fountain pen. Stamped on the back of the clipboard were the words THE INSPECTORATE OF CHILDREN'S INSTITUTIONS.

Nerves dancing in her stomach, Cos did the only thing

that came to mind: she slammed the door shut and drew the door chain across.

'What do we do?' she whispered to the others. They shrugged, wide-eyed.

The woman rapped loudly on the door. 'Excuse me, what is the meaning of this?'

Cos was suddenly unable to form words. Mary sprang towards her, bumping her aside with her hip. With the rattling chain still across, Mary inched open the door, placing an eye in the gap. 'Why, hello! How can we help you?'

Her voice was bright and cheery. It was only from behind that Cos could tell that Mary was in an all-or-nothing battle with her anxiety: her foot tapped on the floor and she shuddered.

Cos heard the lady scoff. 'My name is Miss Seymour, from the Inspectorate of Children's Institutions. I believe a Miss . . . *Meriton* is expecting me.'

Cos grew cold. In all her worry about her father and the stolen painting and Miss Meriton's suspiciously long absence from the Home, she'd completely forgotten about the inspection that the matron had spent so many hours preparing for. She had to say something – *anything* – to make the woman go away until Miss Meriton returned. She eyed the woman, racking her brain for the perfect lie, and nudged Mary aside.

'Unfortunately, Miss Meriton has come down with a sudden highly infectious illness.'

'I'm sorry?' Miss Seymour frowned.

'Miss Meriton – she's ill. In fact . . .' Cos glanced back at the others, raising her eyebrows. 'We all are.'

On cue, the girls began to retch, sneeze and cough so violently that the woman withdrew a handkerchief, placing it across her nose and mouth as though she might also suddenly fall sick.

'This is *most* unusual,' muttered Miss Seymour, her voice muffled by her makeshift face mask. 'Why couldn't Miss Meriton have sent me a letter by return of post?'

'She's barely able to lift her head, never mind write a letter. We all feel awful, and we wouldn't want you to catch this sickness, ma'am.' Cos ended with a hacking cough that scratched painfully at her throat.

'It's suspected influenza, ma'am,' piped up Mary. 'Symptoms should ease in a few days.'

There was a pause that seemed to last forever as the inspector weighed up her options: go into the Home and risk getting ill, or leave with her task incomplete.

'Hmmm,' she said, as though she wasn't entirely convinced.

Cos tried a sickly smile.

'Influenza *is* common in this weather.' She sighed. 'Fine, I shall return for my inspection on Friday at six p.m. sharp.'

'Friday?' Cos squeaked. *That was only two days away. That would be all right, wouldn't it? Plenty of time for Miss Meriton to return.*

The woman nodded primly, scratched an 'X' on to the paper attached to her clipboard and slipped away in the morning light.

CHAPTER ELEVEN

Cos felt as though she was in a nightmare. Her father was in jail, accused of being the Spectre, and now Miss Meriton – who should have been back hours ago – had gone missing.

Cos shook herself. They had to come up with a plan, *now*. Miss Meriton had left the Home to go and find Aggie. Cos knew the matron well enough by now to realise that she would never willingly not return. Something was wrong. Perhaps some unfortunate incident had held both ladies up? With Miss Seymour promising to return in two days, whatever had happened, the girls needed to find both women urgently.

As the entrance foyer filled with worried children, Cos locked eyes with Diya, Mary, Pearl and Miles.

'Girls,' said Mary, in her best impression of Miss Meriton, 'why don't you head to the dormitory and get dressed?'

Slowly but surely, the other girls drifted upstairs, a pouting Dolly taking up the rear. As soon as they were alone, Cos and her friends put their heads together and began to discuss everything.

'If we find Aggie, then we'll find Miss Meriton . . .'

'But where is she? Did Miss Meriton give you any clues as to where she was going, Cos?'

Cos shook her head. 'None.'

'You know who *might* know where Aggie is, though,' ventured Mary.

'Who?'

'The staff at the *London Gazette*,' said Mary matter-of-factly. 'She must've told them all about her latest investigation and where she was going undercover. Their headquarters are on Fleet Street.'

'You're a genius, Mary!' Cos exclaimed. 'That's the first place to look. Can you map us a route to the *Gazette* offices, as fast as possible?'

Mary nodded and disappeared into the Home's library.

'What about the others, Cos?' Diya nodded upstairs, towards the dormitory. 'We ought to tell them where we're going, but I'm afraid that if we do, they'll want to come with us . . .'

Cos thought for a beat. 'We'll tell them the truth – it's only fair. But we'll explain that they should stay here. We need to attract as little attention as possible from the general public, and twenty disabled girls are far more conspicuous than the four of us, plus Miles. We don't want to give Miss Seymour any excuse to return earlier, and if the authorities hear even a whisper about Miss Meriton's disappearance they might insist she be replaced, or – even worse – split up the Home entirely.'

The others nodded in agreement as Mary returned from the library, clutching a tattered bundle of documents. 'The Underground system is so complicated – every company has a different map. Really, there ought to be one. That would make things so much easier. But I *have* plotted us a route to Fleet Street. We need to catch the District line from Kensington station to St Paul's railway station.'

'Miss Meriton keeps an emergency stash of money in her office,' said Pearl. 'There should be enough for tickets for us all.'

Before anyone could stop her, Pearl darted into the matron's office. Footsteps overhead told Cos that the other girls were dressed and ready for the day, and heading back downstairs. As Cos, Mary, Miles and Diya put on their coats, the lift doors dinged open, and a gaggle of girls stampeded down the stairs with wonky ponytails, inside-out dresses and shoes on the wrong feet.

'We're READY!' trilled Dolly, twirling a cerise feather boa

round her neck. Her face fell when she saw the coats and scarves. 'What's going on?'

Before Cos could answer, Pearl shuffled out of Miss Meriton's office, holding a purse.

An uncharacteristic scowl flashed across Dolly's face. 'You're going out and leaving us here? This is *just* like the Treasure Palace Heist – you lot leaving us out again.' There was a murmur of agreement from the girls behind her.

As she blinked at Dolly's scrunched-up face, Cos had never felt more like an adult. She did not like the feeling at all. 'We need to prioritise getting Miss Meriton back before the inspector returns,' she said, before drawing in a deep breath. 'We have to be . . . *sensible* about this.' A shiver ran up Cos's spine. She had never, ever in her life tried to be sensible, or told anyone else to be sensible. It was the opposite of everything she was.

'Hmmm.' Dolly crossed her arms and glared at Cos.

'Cos is right, Dolly.' Miles stepped forward. 'If we all go out, we'll be noticed, and someone is bound to inform the authorities that we've been left home alone.' He plucked a glinting twopenny from the back of Dolly's ear, coaxing a giggle from the girls. 'We'll be back soon, and then we can all work together to find the real Spectre.'

They left the girls in the schoolroom, with Mary directing them to learn about animal predators whilst they were gone.

In spite of the Spectacular's unexpected closure, the streets of Kensington were packed with people. The morning was bright, almost too warm for coats, and the trees were full of pinkish blossoms that drifted on to the sun-dappled pavements.

'Follow me!' Mary was armed with her trusty clipboard, striding purposefully down the street, avoiding other pedestrians with well-practised dodges. 'We're headed for Kensington's Underground station.'

Peering over her shoulder, Cos caught a glimpse of Mary's step-by-step route from the Home to the offices of the *London Gazette*, via a squiggly line that Cos assumed represented the train journey they were going to make. They weaved through a tangle of cobbled streets, passing horse-drawn carriages and street sellers shouting out their wares.

Kensington station was an imposing white brick building bedecked with archways and topped with turrets at each corner. It thronged with travellers, from smart businessmen wearing top hats and carrying handsome briefcases, to fashionably dressed women, to governesses herding their wards. Mary approached the ticket officer with trembling hands, but the man was happy to sell her five third-class tickets. There was no lift, so Diya and Cos struggled down the stairs, with Cos holding tightly to the rail as waves of travellers tried to push past her in their rush to get to the platforms. Miles carried a pink-cheeked Diya, Mary and Pearl folded up her wheelchair and hurried down after them. Sweat beading on her forehead, Cos finally reached the platform alongside her friends, just as the railway tracks began to rattle and a train wheezed towards them, sending a whoosh of air through the station.

Mary chivvied them all into the already packed carriage. Cos found herself squeezed tightly in between Pearl – who had her eyes shut and her hands clamped over her ears – and the padded wall of the train. Cos gritted her teeth as she leaned on the handle of her walking stick, staring longingly at the passengers who had managed to secure seats. There was no opportunity for her to talk to her friends; the train was far too crammed and the engine far too noisy for that. The train rocked on the tracks, the gas lighting flickering.

They alighted at St Paul's. Cos slowly tackled another set of stairs before finally catching a glimpse of daylight as they followed the crowd towards the exit.

Mary led them through a warren of back alleys until they reached Fleet Street. In the distance, Cos could just make out the dome of St Paul's, glistening in the morning sunlight. The street itself was bustling, a mixture of offices and taverns lining the pavements.

Mary strode towards a redbrick building, stained slightly grey from the smoke of the nearby factories. Above its grand door sat an arch engraved with leaves, acorns and foliage. A sign read **THE LONDON GAZETTE**. Cos wilted a little, her breath coming out in puffs.

'Well done, Mary,' Miles said, clapping her on the back. 'Let's go and find our lady journalist!'

CHAPTER TWELVE

Cos swayed, almost knocking Pearl off balance as pain shot up her leg. Their walk and the many stairs in the Underground had made her joints feel very unsteady. Cos fought to stay upright as Miles pushed open the door.

They found themselves in a small but bustling office, cloaked by a thick cloud of tobacco smoke. Waving away the fog, Cos saw that they were at the back of a queue of people, all clutching copies of the *London Gazette*. At the front of the queue a tiny fur-swathed lady was shouting at a black-suited gentleman with a fuzz of mutton-chop whiskers.

'I conducted a seance at Kensington Town Hall two nights ago, after I had left my show at the Spectacular, on behalf of the British Spiritualist Society. I arrived at midnight precisely and spent the next twenty-four hours communing with spirits,' the angry lady spluttered. 'But it appears that a so-called journalist infiltrated our sacred meeting and printed LIES about it in your newspaper. I demand an immediate retraction.' She emphasised this point by thwacking a copy of the *Gazette* on the shining mahogany desk.

Cos caught a glimpse of the headline that had so enraged the lady: *MEDIUM'S TRICKERY EXPOSED: GHOST TALKING IS A HOAX!* She peered at the lady. Something about her seemed familiar, somehow.

'Madame Kaplinsky, please calm down,' pleaded the man.

Ah, thought Cos, *that's why she's familiar – she's the ghost whisperer from the Spectacular.*

Behind the desk, the walls were lined with shelves stuffed with folders. The latest edition of the *London Gazette* was pasted against the back wall, the headlines screaming *THE SPECTACULAR TO REOPEN TOMORROW FOR ITS FINAL DAY: EVENT REFUSES TO BE DAUNTED BY THE SPECTRE'S COWARDLY THEFT. PAINTING STILL NOT FOUND; THIEF PROTESTS HIS INNOCENCE. MIDNIGHT MASQUERADE TO GO AHEAD AS PLANNED.*

Cos bristled. The newspaper had just accepted that her dad was the Spectre with no evidence, even though he was supposed to be innocent until proven guilty! The system seemed broken beyond repair. She felt a new surge of pride that her mother had campaigned so tirelessly for prison reform.

'Psst,' Miles whispered, pointing towards a small, unobtrusive plaque affixed to a frosted glass door. It read *Editorial Dept.* 'Reckon we should skip the queue and go straight to Aggie's desk?'

Cos glanced back at the angry woman, who seemed no closer to finishing her tirade. They couldn't afford to waste any time. She nodded at Miles. Before they could dart towards it, the door to the Editorial Department swung open and two guffawing men strode out. Quick as a wink, Miles caught the door on his shoe, and the group slipped inside.

Ahead was a large room crammed full of desks stacked high with paper and clouded with thick swirls of tobacco smoke. Perched at each desk were harried-looking women, each frantically *tap-tap-tapping* on typewriters. At the far end of the room were hulking black machines – Cos supposed they were printers.

In the centre of the room, a group of men clustered, staring in awed silence as a blustering mountain of a man boomed at them, using his cigar to point at a board covered in newspaper clippings, handwritten notes and pencil sketches of various faces, all connected with pins and string. With a sharp intake of breath, Cos realised it was an investigation board, just like the one she and her friends had put together to plan the Treasure Palace Heist and delve into Lord Fitzroy's past.

At the top of the board, written in shaky, almost illegible handwriting, was the title THE SPECTRE. Bullet points were written underneath the moniker:

- International thief of all types of valuables and artefacts, with an especial preference for one-of-a-kind, priceless and rare items.
- Leaves a calling card at each of his crime scenes in place of the stolen article.
- Master of disguise.

Before Cos could ask her to, Mary was scribbling down the contents of the board.

Cos drew closer to get a better look at what was underneath the bullet points. Each charcoal sketch of a face had been pinned next to a card with a location printed across it, and photos of some of the most beautiful things Cos had ever seen – from rings to gold coins to paintings to jewels. The string zigzagged all the way from years-ago heists, to the Spectre's more recent targets. And, now that Cos had got closer, she could make out that the handwritten notes were actually detailed police reports. This was amazing! This was a treasure trove. This was . . . *being taken down?*

A short, suited man was balancing precariously on a chair, unpinning every document and lobbing it into a wastepaper bin at the side of the board.

And to Cos's absolute horror, in place of the carefully curated investigation into a criminal mastermind, he pinned a photo of . . .

'Father?'

A younger Edmund stared back at Cos, his anger and sadness recorded forever in time. He glared at the photographer, tattoo-less arms crossed.

It must've been taken, thought Cos, *the very first time he went to prison – for stealing food to feed his siblings.* He was only a handful of years older than her in the photo. She could trace their matching crooked eyebrows, and the freckles that also dotted her cheeks. Cos felt herself drift towards the photo, stomach clenched painfully, trying to memorise every inch of the slightly blurred image: from the mess of his hair to the board of random numbers held just below his chin.

Above the photo a question had been scrawled on another pinned piece of paper: *WHO IS EDMUND DEANS, AKA THE SPECTRE?* And spiralling off was a series of answers that struck ire into Cos's belly:

Ex-con, long record, history of stealing.

Experienced in sewing: essential, given the Spectre's many disguises.

Guttersnipe upbringing: all family dead apart from one crippled child.

Before she could stop herself, Cos hurried to the board

and, snarling, ripped down the horrible pieces of paper and crumpled them into rubbish. There was a collective intake of breath from the gathered men.

'No, Cos!' shouted Diya.

'Well, who do we have here then?' asked the huge man, peering down at Cos as if she was an enigma to be unravelled. He didn't – like his colleagues – look utterly aghast at the children who had just stormed into his office, but instead he seemed curious, in a way that made Cos feel itchy. He had a very impressive moustache and ginger whiskers that tickled the corners of his eyes, which he narrowed at the children.

'Mr Milner, did I just hear "Cos"?' asked one of the other men, flicking through a tiny notebook. 'As in, Cosima? That's the name of the child – the Spectre's child.'

Cos felt her cheeks burn as every adult turned to stare at her.

'Did you know he was a criminal?' asked one.

'Do you know where he's hidden his ill-gotten gains?' shouted another.

'Can we take a picture?' said someone else. Before Cos could speak, a flash blinded her momentarily.

'He's not the Spectre,' she growled, the camera light dancing behind her eyes.

'He blooming well is,' said one of the men. 'He was caught red-handed. And when they searched his accommodation police found future disguises for the Spectre.'

Cos heard Mary's sharp intake of breath before she was able to process what the man had said. *The police had searched Edmund's flat and found more evidence that suggested he was the thief?* Her heart thudded. Whoever the Spectre really was seemed determined to frame her dad. All of a sudden, Cos felt utterly hopeless.

'Quiet!' shouted Mr Milner – whom Cos assumed was the editor of the *Gazette*. He waved his cigar at the journalist, who immediately clamped his mouth shut. 'Don't tell her anything unless she gives us some titbits on the Spectre.'

'I-I'm here to see Agatha de la Dulce,' Cos stammered. 'Is she here? Wait, she didn't help with–' Cos waved her hand towards the investigation board – '*this*, did she?'

'Pah, she wishes!' one of the gathered newsmen guffawed. 'Lady journalists like her don't have the wherewithal to put together such a complicated and comprehensive analysis of all the evidence.'

At least that's something, thought Cos. *Of course Aggie isn't involved in the crude and insulting frame-up of my father.*

The editor turned back to Cos, looming over her like a ghoul, with what Cos supposed was intended to be a friendly smile, but it was all teeth. 'Now, little girl,' he simpered, 'if you want information on the lady journalist, it isn't going to come for free. You've got to give me something back. That's the way the world works.'

Rage bubbled up in Cos, but before she could spit more venom the man's way there was an insistent tug on her hand. Pearl laced her fingers round Cos's, and the sudden touch gave Cos a second to think things through. She bit her lip.

'One question and answer about my father is worth one question and answer about Aggie,' she muttered.

A wide smile cracked Mr Milner's ruddy face. 'You're a fast learner,' he exclaimed disbelievingly. 'I'll go first. Did your father raise you?'

Cos's cheeks burned again. She was sure that the question was a trick one – they already knew that Edmund had spent most of her childhood in prison. Her answer would only be used to damn him even more. She glanced round at the men, their eyes trained on her, pencils poised above notepads, and sighed. Out of the corner of her eye she saw Mary tiptoe towards the overflowing bin beneath the investigation board, and begin to pick up discarded pieces of paper. Cos had to keep the men's attention on her.

'No,' she muttered.

'Say again?' boomed the editor. 'Did your father raise you?'

'No,' Cos repeated, her voice strained. The word felt like a betrayal of the worst kind. 'I have a disability, so I was raised in a Home with my friends.' The men began to scribble in their notebooks. 'Now it's my turn. Where's Aggie?'

Mr Milner straightened, resting his hands on his stomach.

'No idea. She's probably off on another one of her crusades – righting wrongs and saving the vulnerable.' He sounded dismissive.

'That's not a proper answer!' Miles said angrily.

The editor shrugged. 'I didn't say it would be a fair bargain, but it's the truth. That woman has been more trouble than she is worth. She is . . . *bloody difficult.*'

There was a chorus of agreement from the other men.

'She's probably licking her wounds,' guffawed the man with the camera. 'Last time I saw her, she was convinced she was about to crack the Spectre case – all on her own, when the best detectives in the world couldn't catch him.'

'Aggie was conducting an independent investigation into the Spectre case?' asked Diya. That seemed important somehow, although Cos couldn't work out why.

'Every journalist worth their salt was working on the Spectre case,' another man said.

'Oi, don't be giving her the goods for free,' growled Mr Milner. 'My turn. Is your father skilled at dressmaking?'

It was such an innocuous question that Cos was momentarily stunned into silence.

'Oh, he's the very best,' exclaimed Pearl. 'He's even taught me new techniques.'

The men began to scribble again. Pearl's expression morphed into horror. She mouthed a 'sorry' at Cos. Cos felt as if she was a fly caught in Mr Milner's trap. This wasn't how Aggie did journalism at all, and Cos didn't like it one bit.

'Your go,' said the editor with a smarmy smile.

He already thinks he's won, Cos thought mutinously, and he kind of had – if what he was saying was true, and he didn't know where Aggie was, then their trip here had been entirely pointless.

Cos thought hard before deciding which question to ask. 'Where is Aggie's desk?'

Mr Milner gestured with his thumb. 'Back there, nearest to the printers. Boys, back to your desks. I think we have tomorrow's front page. And, Bertie,' he added, glancing towards the reedy man hovering at the board, 'fix this.'

He gestured to the pile of papers Cos had torn down. Quick as a wink, Cos slipped the younger photo of her dad into her pinny pocket. Even though it had been horrid to see it pinned up, surrounded by all those untruths, Cos had never seen a picture of her dad before, and she was going to treasure it. As she did so, Cos noticed that Mary had managed to empty the wastepaper bin completely. The *Gazette*'s discarded investigation into the Spectre was now in the hands of Cos and her friends.

The journalists hurried back to their desks. Cos shouted her final question over the din. 'Can we see Aggie's desk?'

Mr Milner shrugged. 'Fine by me. There's nothing of

interest there. When you do find her, tell her I need to speak to her. I'm fed up with this constant need to go off-piste – if she can't toe the *Gazette* line, she'll need to find another editor to write for. She should be covering lady issues – fashion, society and the like.'

Cos swallowed. Aggie's journalism career was everything to her, and even though the *Gazette* offices were full of smoke and loud men, Cos knew she would be devastated to know that her job hung in the balance. As she turned to head towards Aggie's desk, he added, 'She's a funny one. I'd be wary if I were you.'

Cos frowned. What did he mean?

CHAPTER THIRTEEN

Cos's friends began to ply her with questions.

'What do we do now, Cos?'

'Do you think they'll make us have the Stains back?'

'Where is Miss Meriton?' Pearl was on the verge of tears. 'If Aggie's editor doesn't know where she is, maybe the matron couldn't find her either . . .'

Cos didn't have any answers, so she was silent as she slowly picked her way towards the desk closest to the hulking printers. She wondered how on earth Aggie managed to get any work done at all with the constant droning echoing in her ears. Unlike the other desks, Aggie's desk wasn't a state. A battered typewriter sat next to a framed photo of the girls from the Star Diamond Home and a small wooden stationery organiser. But there were no clues to where Aggie was, or any

123

information about her investigation into the Spectre.

Inky fingerprints were all over the desk. Cos traced a thumbprint with her finger, wishing the real Aggie was this close to her. But at that moment Aggie seemed further away than when she'd been on the other side of the world, travelling the globe at the behest of the *Gazette*.

Cos collapsed into Aggie's desk chair, which squeaked ominously. She tried to ignore the spiralling dread in her stomach, and buried her head in her hands. 'Urgh, there's nothing here,' she moaned.

'I wouldn't say nothing.' Miles lifted a hole punch out of the small wooden storage box and knocked his fist against the bottom. 'Hollow,' he muttered, pushing down on a corner. 'A false bottom.' He pulled out a wrinkled, ripped piece of paper. Slowly he unfolded it, laying it flat on the desk. The handwriting was so messy that Cos could barely make out the shiver-inducing words:

AGREE TO MY DEMANDS OR I WILL EXPOSE YOUR SECRET FOR ALL THE WORLD TO SEE

A threat. A threat that Aggie had hidden away. But who had threatened her? And what secret did she want to protect?

'I wonder what was written below the rip?' Diya's fingers traced the jagged edge of the note. 'Maybe the blackmailer said more about what they wanted?'

'Do you think this has anything to do with Aggie's undercover investigation?' Mary whispered breathlessly. 'Or her hunt for the Spectre?'

Cos swallowed. 'I don't know.'

More mysteries. Another unanswerable question. After searching Aggie's desk and finding nothing else of note, Cos picked up the paper, carefully folding it and placing it in her pinny pocket. She drifted back through the *Gazette* offices in a daze, a few steps behind her friends. But as she approached the exit she heard something that made her ears prick up.

'Bertie, get down to West London Magistrates Court and Police Station. The Spectre is being transported to Newgate this afternoon,' barked Mr Milner. 'See if we can get a comment from him.'

Cos felt her stomach drop. Her father was being moved to prison. Maybe she could go to the court and ask him if he knew anything that might help them find the real Spectre? He had been strangely quiet after they'd found out about the theft. And even if he had no clue about who'd framed him, at least she could be a friendly face for him to see on his way to Newgate.

They slipped out of the *Gazette* offices, unnoticed by the journalists hunched over their desks.

When they passed the newspaper boy in the street, Cos stopped to buy the latest edition of the *Gazette*. The headline felt like a stab to her heart. There was confirmation of what she'd just overheard:

After an appearance at the West London Magistrates Court and Police Station, the Spectre is expected to be transferred to a London lock-up, in anticipation of his criminal trial later this year.

Cos swore to herself that she was going to find the real Spectre and make him pay for what he'd done.

CHAPTER FOURTEEN

The train journey back to the Home was silent. Cos sat, her thoughts swirling, trying to make sense of everything:

Someone had framed her father for crimes Cos was sure he hadn't committed. Edmund Deans *couldn't* be the Spectre, but the police didn't seem to care that they'd put the wrong person in prison.

Aggie had been investigating the Spectre and, according to one of her colleagues, had been sure that she was about to crack the case. But the only thing they'd found on her desk was a threatening note.

Miss Meriton, Aggie's closest companion and the only person who knew where Aggie was, had vanished in her search for the lady journalist. *That is the only explanation for her continued absence from the Home*, Cos thought, *and it probably means that both women are in trouble.* And if Miss Meriton didn't return in time for the inspection in two days, then the authorities might close the Home.

Her friends were also distracted. As they approached the Home, Cos's stomach tightened with nerves. They were about to return home *without* the matron. Mary must have been feeling similarly nervy: her hands shook as she unlocked the front door. As Cos limped inside, she was so focused on how she was going to break the news about Miss Meriton gently to the girls that she almost failed to notice the destruction that greeted them.

Almost.

Streams of multicoloured toilet paper hung from the ceiling, trailing round lights and the rickety banister. The walls were covered in crayon drawings and even the paintings on display hadn't escaped – the portrait of Miss Meriton's mother now sported a curled moustache. Marbles were scattered across the floor. Open-mouthed, Cos stepped further into the entrance foyer, almost impressed by how the girls – left alone for a few hours and no longer terrified of their matron – had transformed the building into their imagination's paradise and every adult's worst nightmare.

Her feelings quickly changed when she stepped in a puddle that seemed to be spreading from the nearby lavatory. Cos leaned on her walking stick as she bent down to peel a sodden piece of paper off the sole of her shoe. She peered at the dripping paper. It looked like an old document. Cos frowned at it, struggling to make out some of the words.

TH OME R UN ORT NATE GIRLS
NO R ND R D, KE S NG ON
RUL S

A bit further down, the page was only slightly damp, and Cos could see the words a little better.

No child can be received whose medical certificate has not been examined and approved by a doctor.
MEDICAL CERTIFICATE

Cos had seen a certificate like this before – in fact, she *had* one. Every girl living at the Home did. It was proof of their disability.

Back when the Stains were in charge, Cos had seen countless medical certificates signed by doctors who barely shot a disdainful look at a girl before deeming her 'hopelessly crippled'. Maybe that was why the sight of the florid handwriting of a long-ago doctor made her feel so worried.

More papers were scattered across the floor, and she ducked to pick up some. There were more medical certificates, and admission papers and letters from way before her time.

'What on earth—' began Diya, as the spokes of her wheelchair got caught in a soggy clump of documents.

'EN GARDE!' Dolly yelled triumphantly, bursting into the entrance foyer, holding a walking stick as though it were a sword. She had orange stripes painted wonkily on her cheek, wore a hat she had clearly borrowed from the coat stand and was followed by a gaggle of other girls, all dressed similarly. One girl, Clementine, carried a makeshift flag constructed from a crutch and a nightdress, a tiger painted on it.

Dolly spun towards Cos like a tornado, then came to an abrupt stop when she realised who Cos was. She dropped her walking stick/sword, abashed. 'Oh, Cos, you're back,' she said, peering behind Cos to look for Miss Meriton. 'We thought you'd be longer.'

'Why did you get all these out?' Cos waved her bundle of old Home documents.

Dolly shrugged. 'Miss Meriton said our history was important, so we wanted to look at the lives of some of the girls who came before us. Did you know that the matron before Miss Stain was called Miss Whymper? What a name!'

Next to Cos, Mary, who couldn't stand anything being messy or disorganised, vibrated with anxiety.

Suddenly there was another sound, this time from the direction of the kitchen.

BUUP BUPP BUUP BUURRRRPPPPP!

Cos frowned. It had sounded a little like a trumpet fanfare, the kind used at very fancy events.

Then the kitchen doors were kicked open. A group of girls burst into the entrance foyer, led by a girl called Maud, who had ingeniously turned her hearing trumpet into an *actual* trumpet. Like Dolly's group, Maud's also had a flag – theirs had a drawing of a shark on it.

With the appearance of the rival group, Dolly and her

friends seemed to bristle. Swords were raised aloft and shouts were exchanged:

'TIGERS TO VICTORY!'

'NO! SHARKS ARE BETTER!'

Diya finally managed to remove the clump of paper from her spokes and wheeled forward to separate the two groups. 'What is going on?' she shouted, shooting her sternest glare at the girls. 'You were supposed to be in the schoolroom learning about predators!'

Dolly looked a little sheepish. 'Well, we *were*,' she explained. 'But then *she* –' Dolly pointed her sword at Maud – 'started an argument by saying that sharks were the most fearsome predator, when everyone sensible knows that it's tigers.'

Dolly's statement was met with a murmur of agreements and protests. Mary, who was still shivering in silent rage, finally regained her voice. 'That doesn't explain all of *this*.' She waved her hand at the disarray.

'We started arguing, but we were getting nowhere,' Maud muttered. 'So we thought we'd split into teams to determine who was the most fearsome animal. We decorated the building to be like the climates that tigers and sharks live in.' She pointed at the greenish swirl of toilet paper nearest to her. 'Some tigers live in rainforests,' she explained. 'And we attempted to recreate the ocean for the sharks.' She pointed at the puddle. 'But something went wrong with the pipes.'

Mary began to pace back and forth across the foyer. 'So the whole Home looks like this?'

There was a pause, before all the girls nodded.

'Oh, goodness,' Mary said.

'Where's Miss Meriton?' asked Sybil suddenly. 'And Aggie?'

The air seemed to leave the room in a whoosh. The fierceness of the girls' argument dissipated, leaving them looking confused and worried.

Cos sighed, and set down the old Home papers on the comfy armchair. She couldn't lie to the girls. 'We can't find them. Aggie or Miss Meriton.'

A gasp echoed through the entrance foyer. In seconds, all the makeshift weapons had been abandoned, all arguments about tigers and sharks forgotten.

'They're *lost*?' Dolly's bottom lip wobbled.

Cos gave the barest of nods. 'But we're going to get them back – both of them – before that inspector comes back.' Cos hoped she sounded more confident than she felt.

'In two days?' Maud asked disbelievingly.

'Actually, it's one and a half now,' added Pearl, unhelpfully.

Defiance surged through Cos. 'YES!' she almost roared. *Yes, yes, yes, yes* echoed through the foyer. 'We may not have found Aggie and Miss Meriton today, but we did find some clues that will help us get them back *and* prove my father isn't the Spectre. And I think everything might be connected.'

Dolly wiped away her tears and crooked a curious eyebrow. 'How?'

They gathered in the schoolroom, where the blackboard that used to be hidden in their dormitory had been relocated following the Stains' departure. The classroom, like the whole Home, also looked as if it had been hit by a hurricane, with upended chairs, scattered crayons and pieces of screwed-up paper all over the floor.

Dolly turned to Cos. 'Tell us everything.'

Quickly, Cos explained what had happened when they had visited the *Gazette* offices. Mary flicked open her satchel, plucked out the crinkled papers she had taken from the wastepaper bin, and began to pin them to the blackboard. Once they were all in place, Cos grabbed some chalk and wrote out, in her spidery handwriting, the bullet points that had been scribbled across the *Gazette*'s board.

Soon, they had recreated the *Gazette*'s entire investigation into the Spectre.

'It looks as though an entirely different person committed each theft,' Dolly suggested, pointing at the various sketches of each suspect. The thief of the diamond necklace had a bushy beard, a beret balanced jauntily on his head and a wrinkled face. The lady who had infiltrated the fancy ball in New York was young, glamorous and wearing a sparkly gown.

The violin-nabber was a freckle-faced teenager masquerading as a maid. And the crook who stole *The Lady Invalid* had a distinctive polka-dot necktie.

'Mmhmmmmmm,' said Mary, her mouth still full of pins.

'What I think Mary is trying to say is that the Spectre is a master of disguise,' explained Diya. 'That's one of the reasons they think Cos's father is the thief. He is a brilliant tailor.'

Cos paused as a realisation hit her. 'He's been making costumes all week for that Midnight Masquerade thingy – that's why the police found costumes in his flat. They weren't for the Spectre – they were for guests at the ball.'

'The Spectre seems to revel in chaos,' said Pearl, gazing at the board. 'He's committed multiple thefts for years, all different items, from gemstones to musical instruments to art, and the only clue linking each crime is his calling card.'

'Did you find anything else at the *Gazette* offices?' Dolly asked.

'Yes!' Mary said, retrieving the note from her satchel. 'A threat.'

'A threat?' Maud's voice quivered.

'We found it on Aggie's desk. It wasn't signed, or very specific – but it suggests that Aggie is in some sort of trouble,' Miles explained. Mary pinned it on the blackboard. The scrawled words sent shivers down Cos's spine again.

AGREE TO MY DEMANDS OR I WILL EXPOSE YOUR SECRET FOR ALL THE WORLD TO SEE

'What's Aggie's secret?' Dolly asked.

Cos sighed. 'I'm not sure. The only secrets Aggie has ever kept from us are ones relating to her work. We know she's investigating something undercover. Maybe someone's found out that she's not who she says she is.'

'Do you think she could be in danger?' Ida signed, clutching her favourite doll close to her chest. *'Her and Miss Meriton? Do you think the Spectre has them?'*

Cos thought for a beat. Aggie had told her colleagues that she was close to unmasking the true identity of the Spectre – had she got too close? 'Maybe,' she conceded. 'In fact, I think it's highly likely.'

'So what do we do, Cos?' Maud's eyes brimmed with tears. 'The inspector is due back in a couple of days, and we've got no matron.'

'Simple,' Cos said as she turned back to their investigation board. 'We find Miss Meriton and Aggie, clear my father's name *and* catch the real Spectre, all before Miss Seymour returns.'

Cos's announcement sparked a chorus of theory-swapping and wild ideas about how they would actually achieve these lofty goals (her personal favourite was Dolly's, who suggested that they trick the Spectre into robbing the Home by telling the whole of London they had an attic full of gold). She stared at the investigation board until the crime-scene photos and drawings of stolen items blurred together.

Without warning, she shot to her feet, her joints protesting with a series of painful clicks. 'Sitting here talking won't get us anywhere. We HAVE to do something. Let's go to the Spectacular now – and see if the real Spectre left any clues to their identity.' She stormed out of the schoolroom and towards the entrance foyer, her walking stick tapping loudly on the floor. The others followed her.

'I admire your spontaneity, Cos,' squeaked Mary, holding her clipboard close to her chest, 'but going to the Spectacular right now gives me no time to assess potential pitfalls or plan our route.'

'I saw you wince when you stood up, *and* I heard your joints creak something awful,' Diya muttered furiously. 'You need to rest, not go gallivanting around London.'

Cos ignored them, and put on her coat and scarf.

'What about us?' demanded Dolly, her arms crossed. 'What do you want us to do? I don't want to be left out this time.'

The other girls murmured their agreement. 'We want our own mystery to solve – like you have,' added Maud.

Cos turned towards the front door, only to find her way blocked by a determined-looking Pearl, who held up a familiar newspaper. It was the one Cos had bought outside the *Gazette* offices. Pearl jabbed a headline with the end of her paintbrush.

'The Spectacular doesn't even reopen until tomorrow morning,' Pearl said. 'There's no point in going now – security will have been tightened after the theft. And if you are caught there it will make your father look even more guilty.'

All the fight seemed to drain out of Cos. Pearl was right. She replaced her coat and scarf on the stand. Miles gave her shoulder a sympathetic squeeze. She wouldn't stomp into the Spectacular all guns blazing; she would be sensible and wait. Besides, there was something else she wanted to do this evening . . .

'AHEM!' Dolly coughed. 'What can we do to help?'

Cos racked her mind for a task for the other girls to do that would (a) keep them occupied and (b) not involve the whole building being wrecked. 'Miss Seymour is coming back in less than two days. If the Home isn't perfect, with all those soggy documents tidied away, then there's a huge chance that the authorities will close us down.'

A worried murmur passed through the girls, but Dolly still frowned. 'You want us to *tidy*?' she asked, looking thoroughly unimpressed. 'That sounds like chores . . .'

'It's the most important thing you can do!' Cos insisted. 'You'll be helping to save the Home!'

'Hmmm,' muttered Dolly. She and the other girls had a

whispered discussion. 'Fine, on this occasion and on this occasion *only*, we will tidy. Come on, girls, let's start in the library.' She led the others into the library, and their chorus of grumbles faded away.

Mary smiled gratefully. 'Good idea, Cos.'

'But you do need an early night!' Diya insisted. 'Painkillers and sleep, *now*.' She pointed upstairs.

Cos sighed. There was no use arguing with Diya.

'We visit the Spectacular as soon as it reopens,' Pearl said, folding the newspaper under her arm.

CHAPTER FIFTEEN

B ut Cos didn't go to sleep.

She yawned a goodnight to her friends as she tiptoed into the lift, glancing at the grandfather clock in the entrance foyer as she went. She didn't know exactly when her father was leaving court, just that it was happening this afternoon – she needed to get there as soon as possible.

She made sure she clunked her walking stick loudly down the corridor to the dormitory, where she helped herself to Mary's incredibly detailed homemade map of South Kensington and stuffed her bed with pillows, so that it looked as though she was fast asleep. Then, with some difficulty, she prised open the door to Diya's old invention-station cupboard and pulled out a dusty, cobweb-covered, almost forgotten invention: the Perfect Rappelling Perambulator.

It was a modified version of one of Diya's other inventions, the Wondrous Winch. Attached to one end of the winch was a hand crank, and at its other end was a crude hammock made out of an old bed sheet. Using a length of coiled rope, the hammock could be lowered and lifted by the crank. Cos had last used this contraption when she'd sneaked out of the Home under the noses of the Stain siblings. Back then, her friends had helped. This time she was on her own, which made the whole endeavour a bit trickier.

With a grunt, Cos opened the dormitory window, letting in a breeze that ruffled her tangled hair. Outside, the sky was slate grey and drizzly. Then, holding the perambulator in one hand and her walking stick in the other, Cos sat on the windowsill before swinging her legs round and inching herself, and the contraption, forward on to the narrow ledge outside. The hammock was buffeted by the wind and splattered with rain.

She placed the arm of the perambulator half in and half out of the dormitory window, careful to make sure that the hand crank was on the outside. Then, with an almighty effort, she yanked down the window frame, wedging Diya's creation in place. It looked a little like a crane, with the long wooden arm sticking out at a right angle from the building.

Now came the tricky bits. Cos closed one eye, stuck her tongue out and tried to think with Mary-like precision. Then she threw her walking stick. It landed right on target – in the hammock. Impulsively, Cos cheered, but a violent wobble nearly sent her crashing to the ground. Her heart in her throat, Cos clung to the window ledge as she pulled herself upright. She was barely a pace from the safety of the hammock, but it was swaying this way and that in the wind, and the ground seemed extremely far away.

Cos screwed up her courage, stepping forward into thin air. She landed on her back in the hammock with a thud. For a moment, the hammock rocked and the arm of the perambulator creaked, and Cos had visions of herself tumbling downwards. But then the swaying calmed – and so did Cos's heartbeat.

Using her walking stick, Cos gave the hand crank a firm prod – spinning it so that she and the perambulator hurtled towards the ground. Her fall cushioned by the hammock, Cos clambered out of Diya's excellent contraption and pulled herself upright. She strode into the street, her nose buried in Mary's map. By the time she'd navigated her way to Vernon Street, her breath came in puffs, she had a painful stitch in her side and her knees throbbed with pain. The drizzle had given way to rain that came down in sheets, soaking her.

Under her breath, Cos swore at herself. *I should've brought the Wonderful Wheelchair. And an umbrella.*

Thanks to the driving rain, the street was almost entirely deserted. Only one uniformed policeman stood guard at the front of a redbrick building ringed by wrought-iron railings.

That must be the court and police station, Cos thought.

A lantern above the policeman's head cast a soft glow, the only light on the otherwise gloomy street. As she neared the building, Cos ducked into a shadowy crevice.

From her vantage point, Cos waited, silent and still. Well, as still as Cos could possibly be. Sometimes being stationary somehow made her legs ache even more than dashing around, so every now and then she bent and flexed her legs, just to make sure that every joint was in its right place.

As she huddled there, Detective Constable Wensleydale strode into the building.

Time ticked by. Rain dripped down the nape of Cos's neck. Just as she was beginning to lose hope, a hansom cab pulled up, drawn by two horses. *V. R.* had been painted on the side of the chassis, and the door at the back was barred.

Anticipation thrummed through Cos. She crept as close as she dared, clinging to the railings with one hand and gripping her walking stick with the other. She knew that she would have to be quick, which wasn't something she naturally excelled at. She sucked in a deep breath as the courthouse door opened and a line of bedraggled prisoners – shackled at the wrists and the ankles, and linked together with chains – were led out, escorted by officers. To Cos's horror, children were dotted amongst the unfamiliar men and women, dressed in ragged shirts and holey hats.

She searched the row of people for her father as the first of the prisoners was loaded into the back of the vehicle.

Finally, she spotted him.

He still wore his shabby coat over his Spectacular uniform, but his face was wan and his eyes puffy. She dashed forward without thinking.

'FATHER!'

Edmund's eyes widened, but before he could utter a word the other prisoners began to wriggle away from their escorts, shouting incoherently. Cos's unexpected outburst seemed to have sparked rebellion in them.

'I know you're not the Spectre,' Cos said. Edmund blinked at her. Maybe in all the chaos of the street he hadn't heard her? She cleared her throat and spoke a little louder. 'And I'm going to prove it.'

Edmund frowned at her, not saying anything, as all around them police officers wrestled with the other prisoners.

'Do you have any idea who might have framed you?' Cos cried over the din.

Instead of answering, Edmund plunged his cuffed hands into the pocket of his coat. He pulled something out, mumbling something Cos didn't quite catch, and pressed it into her palms.

'Remember – look to the stars,' he rasped.

A policeman suddenly wrapped his burly arms round

144

Edmund's neck, pulling him to the ground. He tried to shake off the man, but with his wrists and ankles shackled, the police officer soon overpowered him, pinning him face down in the street.

Cos was frozen, staring at her father, unable to do anything to help him, and completely confused by what he had – and hadn't – said.

With an almighty effort, Edmund lifted his head. 'Cos – *go!*'

His commanding tone snapped her out of her daze. All around her pandemonium reigned – prisoners trying to squirm out of their restraints, officers fighting to regain control, horses snorting and kicking, the rain lashing down. It was only a matter of time before more policemen arrived to quell the trouble that she had inadvertently started.

With one last look at her father, Cos turned and limped away as fast as she could. At the end of the street, she ducked round the corner and sheltered from the rain in the portico of a shop so she could examine what her father had given her.

She opened her fists, then gasped. Edmund had passed her two of his most precious possessions: the locket he normally wore on a chain round his neck, and his moon-shaped sewing kit normally kept in his costumier's bag. But why had he given them to her?

'Look to the stars,' Cos whispered to herself. That's what Edmund had said. It was her mother's saying: *Keep your feet on the ground, but always remember to look to the stars.* But how did that relate to the sewing kit and locket? Or proving his innocence?

She clicked open the case, running her fingers across the glinting tools her father used on a daily basis: scissors and needles and an ornate thimble embossed with stars. They were beautiful, but Cos didn't understand how they would help her. A small stack of paper had been folded neatly and tucked into a small leather pouch within the case. The first piece of paper she unfurled was so thin it was almost transparent. It was cut into a familiar square and rough to the touch. Stamped in the corner of the square were the words *H. M. PRISON WORMWOOD SCRUBS*, and faint curling handwriting covered the rest of it.

Cos frowned. 'Prison issue toilet paper?'

She held it up

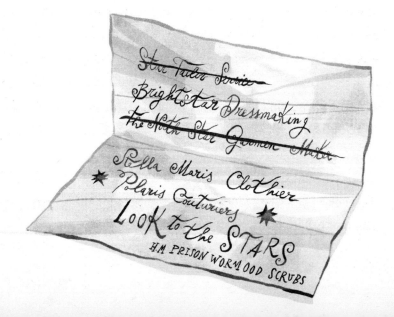

Wonky stars were drawn round the final two words: Polaris Couturiers. They were, Cos realised, ideas for what to call his dream business – ideas he'd confided to Mina, and the reason why a sewing kit was her final gift to him. He must have started to plan his future from his cell.

At the very bottom of the square, written in wobbly typeface, was Edmund's best impression of a business letterhead:

Polaris Couturiers
Look to the STARS

'Cosima!'

Cos spun round, half terrified and half hopeful, plunging the locket and sewing kit safely in her pocket. Most people only used her full name when she was in trouble, and most of the time when she was in trouble Miss Meriton was the one to tell her off. She harboured a wild hope that somehow the matron had come back, but instead a furious Diya – doing a very good impression of a furious Miss Meriton – leaned out from the carriage of a taxi cab.

'Get in here. Now,' she hissed between gritted teeth.

Heart pounding, Cos traipsed over to the cab, her father's gifts weighing heavy in her pinny pocket. Although she was trembling with rage, Diya deployed her ramp to help Cos up the steep stairs to the coach. Inside, in varying states of anger, admiration and worry, were Miles, Mary and Pearl.

Cos sat. 'How did you know where I was?' she asked in a small, not-at-all-Cos-like voice.

'Logical deduction,' Diya muttered curtly, her face like thunder. She snatched Cos's walking stick, tapped the carriage ceiling and the cab jolted forward.

'You went without telling us.' Pearl sniffed, her gaze fixed on her shoes. 'For one moment, when I drew back your blanket, I thought . . . I thought you'd left us. Run away.'

Shame rose in Cos's chest. 'I'd never do that, Pearly. Never ever. I just – I *had* to see my father to ask if he knew who'd framed him. I thought it might help us find the real Spectre.'

'Then why didn't you say anything?' Mary squeaked, tears welling in her eyes.

'Yes – we could've helped,' muttered Miles. 'Or gone together.'

Cos squirmed uncomfortably.

'She was looking after number one again,' Diya said coldly, her disapproval clear even in the shadowy cab. 'Weren't you, Cos? It's not just you that'll be affected if we don't catch the Spectre. If we're right, and the Spectre is involved with Miss Meriton and Aggie's disappearance, then we don't have a matron. And if we don't have a matron then the authorities will close our—' Diya stopped suddenly, a sob replacing her words.

She didn't have to finish her sentence. The gravity of what was at stake for everyone was clear. Cos leaned forward, grabbing Diya's hand. 'I'm sorry, Diya – and to you all. It was awful of me to sneak out without telling you. We're a team, and me going off on my own was selfish.'

Diya wiped her tears on her sleeve. 'It's all right. We know what you're like. Just don't do it again, promise?'

There was a lump in Cos's throat. 'Promise.'

'So, *did* your father have any idea who the Spectre might be?' Mary asked.

Cos had briefly considered keeping her father's gift to herself, but that seemed silly now. Diya was right – they were in this together. And she would need her friends' smarts and creativity if she was going to work out the clue.

'He doesn't look like he's slept, and we didn't get much time to chat,' Cos admitted as she pulled the locket and sewing kit from her pocket. 'All he did was hand me these, and tell me to "look to the stars" – whatever that means.' She passed the sewing kit to Diya, who opened it on her lap. Then Cos carefully clasped her father's locket round her neck, tucking it beneath her dress.

'It's just needles and thread and old orders,' Diya exclaimed, her anger and sadness replaced by curiosity at yet another mystery. 'What does it all mean?'

Cos shrugged. 'I don't know.'

'Maybe he entrusted it to you for safekeeping?' Mary suggested.

'That could be it,' Miles said thoughtfully, tapping his chin. 'It's only when you get transferred to prison that the guards take your clothes and possessions. For whatever reason, Edmund didn't want the guards getting their hands on these things.'

Cos frowned, staring at the moon box as Diya carefully closed it. As sensible as her friends' suggestions seemed, she was sure they hadn't stumbled across the real reason yet. Her father had given her a problem to solve, and she was sure it related to the Spectre somehow.

Outside, the driver knocked smartly on the roof as the coach slowed. 'We're 'ere,' he shouted.

They all clambered out on to their street, wheelchairs and walking sticks in tow. Mary paid their fare. Cos shivered in her damp uniform. The rain had finally let up, but there was a chill in the air, and the crooked rooftops of Kensington were cast in shadows and darkness.

Tomorrow morning they would head to the Spectacular again. Cos only hoped they'd uncover clues that made more sense than the ones Edmund had pressed into her hand.

CHAPTER SIXTEEN

Morning brought grey skies and more rain; the street below the dormitory window jostled with drizzle-slicked umbrellas. Cos felt as gloomy as the weather as she traipsed to the lift with her father's sewing-kit. She hadn't slept well. The Spectre haunted her dreams, an insubstantial ghost of a villain that vanished every time Cos neared, and she was no closer to understanding the sewing-kit clue.

Deciding that the puzzle would never be solved on an empty belly, Cos slipped the sewing-kit into her pocket and made a brief detour to the kitchen for some breakfast. The Home was now a curious mix of Miss-Meriton-level orderliness and unsupervised-girl chaos: the foyer floor was as polished as a gemstone, but remnants of coloured paper and discarded tiger and shark costumes lay here and there. Cos followed a burble of chatter along the corridor and into the schoolroom, toast in hand.

The girls had set up several workstations in their efforts to get the old Home paperwork in order: a few were drying still-damp documents over the roaring fire, then sorting them by year, before finally they were hole-punched and placed in cracked-leather folders.

Miles, Diya and Pearl were peering at Diya and Miles's latest project: silent fireworks. Pearl – who loved seeing the lights dancing across the night sky, but detested the bangs and crashes as they exploded – wore her trusty ear defenders, for good reason. The inventor and magician hadn't *quite* perfected the 'silent' element of their new contraption yet.

'Oof,' Marnie exclaimed from by the fire, waving two documents at Cos. 'This Miss Whymper makes Miss Stain look like an angel. She had a hand in sending this poor girl to a reformatory for stealing food for her friends.'

When the Stains had been in charge, the girls had been fed lumpy gruel and mouldy scraps of bread, so nabbing the expensive sweet treats the stingy siblings kept for themselves gave the girls a glimmer of brightness amidst the gloom. But as bad as the Stains had been, as far as Cos knew, they'd *never* conspired to send a girl to a reformatory. Reformatories were prisons for criminal children, places where judges sent only the most disorderly. Cos shivered as she took the papers from Marnie and read:

THE HOME FOR UNFORTUNATE GIRLS
NORTH END ROAD, KENSINGTON

Copy

11th November 1888

Dear Mr R. P. Haversham Esquire, JP,

You have graciously asked for my opinion before you make a final decision on whether to commit Eunice Reynard to a reformatory school. Eunice has been in my care since her mother relinquished custody in 1886. She is a troublesome child, and her influence on my other charges was altogether undesirable. After she ran away from my establishment last month, I discovered that she had been stealing food for the other children, planning mischievous pranks for her own amusement and frequently forgetting her unfortunate nature.

I fervently believe that sending Eunice to a reformatory is the only suitable option left to discourage her from the path of crime and idleness she is currently on.

Yours truly,
Miss Whymper (Matron of the Home for Unfortunate Girls)

Cos turned to the next paper, which was a court order.

HAMMERSMITH POLICE COURT
METROPOLITAN POLICE DISTRICT,
TO WIT

BE IT REMEMBERED that on the 14th day of November 1888, in pursuance of the Industrial School Act, 1866, I, the undersigned, one of the magistrates of the Police Courts of the Metropolis, sitting at the Police Court Hammersmith within the said District, do order that Eunice Reynard of North End Road, Kensington (whose religious persuasion appears to me to be Protestant), being a child subject to the provisions of section 16 of the said Act, be sent to the girls reformatory at Clerkenwell, London. She should be detained there until she attains the age of sixteen years, she being now the age of eleven years.

R. P. Haversham

Magistrate

Cos's throat felt dry, and her heart clattered against her ribcage. This poor girl – Eunice – had been condemned to a reformatory for five whole years for her Cos-esque exploits. She tore her eyes from the court order and passed the pieces of paper to Ida, who filed them in the 1888 folder.

'Is everyone ready?' Cos asked, pushing all thoughts of the Home's horrid past to the back of her brain.

Four yeses answered her question.

Pearl slid off her ear defenders and strode towards Cos, picking up a bundle of fabric on her way. 'I borrowed some material from the sofa in Miss Meriton's office,' she said sheepishly. Cos knew that really meant she'd stripped the matron's prized sofa of its velvet, but since she'd done it to save the Home Cos didn't think Miss Meriton would mind that much.

'I've fashioned it into jackets for each of us,' Pearl explained, handing Cos hers. It was downy-soft to the touch and embellished with sparkles. 'They're similar to the uniform the Spectacular staff wear. It'll help us to blend in.'

After putting on their jackets, they bade farewell to the other girls and left the Home. Cos's thoughts whirred. They had to find something at the Spectacular that would clear her father *and* point to the real Spectre – or at least where he'd hidden the stolen painting.

As beautiful as Pearl's faux-Spectacular jackets were, they hardly needed them. When they rounded the corner to Earl's Court, they were greeted by a huge swell of people that stretched as far as the eye could see. It seemed the travelling fair was busier than ever. Even the drab grey skies and persistent drizzle hadn't kept the crowds away on the Spectacular's final day. As Cos and her friends elbowed their way through, she caught snippets of conversations that told her exactly why so many were so eager to see the Spectacular before it closed.

'What if the Spectre's still haunting the fair?' squealed a small child.

'I can't wait to see the crime scene!' said another. 'What an exciting event!'

'I've got an inkling I know where the Spectre's hidden the stolen goods,' said a moustachioed man confidently. 'I'm going to tell that fancy sir and collect myself a nice reward.'

The ticket attendants were so busy admitting patrons through the whirring mechanical gates that no one batted an eyelid as Cos and her friends darted behind the queue, slipping into the event the same way they had before: through the gap between the fairground wagons.

Cos was too busy concentrating on putting one foot in front of the other to realise the others had come to a sudden stop. She clattered into the back of Diya's wheelchair and before she could utter an 'ow', Mary had clamped her hand over her mouth.

'Did you hear something?' A stranger's voice cut through the distant queue chatter like a knife.

Cos sucked in a breath as she copied Mary and pressed herself flat against the fairground wagons, hoping they wouldn't be discovered.

The voice seemed to be coming from inside the wagon –

Cos caught a glimpse of two figures through the door, which was ajar.

There was a derisive sigh. 'We have reopened the Spectacular, Theodore – and to great acclaim. Of *course* you can hear something,' replied a man in a pompous voice.

Cos frowned. *Theodore? As in Sir Theodore Vincent – the patron of the Spectacular?*

'I meant something strange,' muttered Sir Vincent.

'You're far too paranoid,' continued the second voice. 'It is most unbecoming of a gentleman.'

Cos realised, with a start, that she'd heard that voice before as well, and recently. *Who was it?*

The man cleared his throat theatrically, and realisation flared in her mind like a torch. She knew who the mystery man was – the Amazing Luminaire!

'Pah! What do you, of all people, know of gentlemanly conduct, Gideon?' Sir Vincent said.

'Enough,' hissed Mr Luminaire. 'What did you find out?'

A tense silence stretched between the two men. Cos listened intently. The only other nearby sound was a curious scratching, as if someone was noting down the conversation. She frowned, glancing back at Mary, but she looked frozen in fear.

'I don't know why you are so fixated by a confounded performer when *The Lady Invalid* is still missing. Father is apoplectic with rage and hasn't slept since—'

There was a sudden smash. Beside Cos, Pearl jumped.

'I don't give a fig about that damned painting!' said Mr Luminaire. 'I want to know that my acts aren't about to be pinched by my competition.'

'Fine,' snapped Sir Vincent. His next words were spoken in barely more than a whisper. 'Gustav left London straight after his performance on Monday. He travelled via train to Dover, where he held a clandestine meeting with representatives from the Barnum & Bailey Circus. He returned to London the next afternoon, in time for Tuesday's show.'

'I knew it! That traitor.' The showman sounded both angry and excited to Cos – a curious mixture of emotions. 'I made his name, and this is how he treats me? We need to plan our revenge – sting that turncoat right where it hurts. I can't afford any more losses.'

Sir Vincent was suddenly struck by a coughing fit. 'I've done all you asked of me,' he said as soon as he regained control. 'Spied on your performers, organised the sham of a masquerade, even persuaded Father to lend you that priceless painting – which will ruin the business if we don't recover it promptly. *Please* return those letters, as you promised you would.'

Mary shifted with discomfort next to Cos. It was troubling to hear Sir Theodore's desperation – and, Cos realised, it very much sounded as though Gideon Luminaire had been blackmailing the art dealer. What was in those letters that had worried him so? And how had Luminaire got his hands on the art dealer's private correspondence?

There was a murmur that Cos didn't quite catch.

'Letters?' said Mr Luminaire, leaving the wagon and clattering down the wagon steps, followed by the art dealer. 'What letters?'

With that, they walked away, still talking, into the Spectacular.

Cos and her friends followed.

CHAPTER SEVENTEEN

A sea of excited visitors were crammed into Earl's Court. Although some were patiently waiting their turn to go on a ride, or queuing up for the delicious food on offer, most, it seemed, were moving towards the Picture Palace. Cos and her friends joined the slow-moving throng. As the gallery finally came into view, the crowd suddenly shuddered to a stop, and a spooky voice drifted towards them.

'Ladies and gentlemen, today I will channel the power of the spirit realm to trace the earthly location of the painting known as *The Lady Invalid*! In doing so, I will prove, once and for all, that mediumship is real! In order to begin, I will need a few volunteers.'

As Cos elbowed her way to the front row, she caught sight of a familiar lady, draped in a velvet cloak and hunched over a crystal ball that sat on a round table. Madame Kaplinsky.

'The first volunteer I need is . . . a gentleman in a tartan raincoat, who has recently lost a great-aunt,' Madame Kaplinsky announced.

There were gasps as a middle-aged man stumbled on to the spiritualist's makeshift stage, blinking in surprise.

'My next volunteer is a widow, long in mourning, wearing a poppy brooch gifted by her beloved.'

A woman at the front of the gathering, her hair streaked with grey, burst into tears. She blew her nose noisily as she stepped up next to the first volunteer, her brooch glinting.

Cos watched, transfixed, as Madame Kaplinsky called up a few more audience members – each of whom the spiritualist knew a seemingly impossible fact about. She gathered the volunteers in a circle round the table, and the audience waited with bated breath.

'Charlatan,' scoffed Diya under her breath from somewhere behind Cos. 'She is peddling unscientific nonsense.'

Madame Kaplinsky frowned. 'I need one more volunteer.' She placed her hands round

the crystal ball, her long nails tapping on its surface, and fell silent for a few heartbeats. 'I'm looking for a young girl who uses a stick to walk, and who has lost her father . . . *twice*.'

Cos sucked in a stunned breath. *That was her – it had to be her. But how did the ghost whisperer know that?* Before she could do or say anything, Pearl had slipped her hand into Cos's and gently pulled her away, back through the crowd.

'Mary says we ought to focus on the task at hand,' the artist murmured, leading Cos towards the Picture Palace.

Cos nodded half-heartedly.

'Don't worry about it, Cos,' Miles insisted as the friends weaved past people. 'Spiritualism is like close-up magic: a clever trick.'

'B-b-but Madame Kaplinsky knew about my father. I lost him once, before I was even born, and now I've lost him again. How could she know that?' Cos felt suddenly adrift from her friends, her heart pounding.

'Lucky guess,' Mary declared matter-of-factly. 'It's Madame Kaplinsky's seance that's *really* interesting. She's saying that she can find *The Lady Invalid* with her supernatural powers.'

Diya snorted.

'You might laugh, Diya, but a medium who tracked down the world's most expensive stolen painting would find herself on the front page of every newspaper,' Mary explained. 'That would be brilliant for her career.'

Cos blinked, her thoughts directed back to the Spectre in an instant. 'You're saying that Madame Kaplinsky might be the real thief?'

Mary shrugged. 'She certainly has a motive.'

They halted at the end of a far shorter queue just before the great glass doors of the Picture Palace. As they waited, Cos's gaze drifted to a poster that had been pasted to a wooden signpost just outside the art gallery.

One corner of the poster was peeling. Absent-mindedly, she pulled at the peeling corner as the queue finally moved forward. Underneath was another poster, advertising the New York Spectacular – where the event had last been. The paper ripped as Cos pulled it, revealing even more poster layers with two more past locations – Paris and Berlin. Something clicked in Cos's mind. *What was it about those places?*

Then Miles called to her from inside the Picture Palace. 'Come on!'

Once inside the marble-floored hall, Cos was immediately struck by how different it looked to the gallery they'd visited only a few days before. Every frame was now empty – the paintings removed, Cos supposed, by anxious owners scared that the Spectre might target their art next. Even though the Picture Palace was now picture-less, it was busier than ever. A dense crowd shuffled slowly towards the far end of the building, eager to see the space where *The Lady Invalid* had formerly resided.

Two new attractions had replaced the priceless works of art. A few Spectacular employees sat at a desk littered with letters and telegrams, and a meandering queue of people lined up to talk to them. A small sign read *INFORMATION ON THE LOCATION OF* THE LADY INVALID.

Next to the sign was a poster, fluttering in the breeze:

METROPOLITAN POLICE
£250 REWARD
STOLEN

between 11.30 p.m. on 12th March and 9.30 a.m. on 13th March from the Spectacular, Earl's Court, London

A PRICELESS WORK OF ART
THE LADY INVALID

The above reward will be paid by Messrs Vincent & Sons to any persons giving such information as will lead to the recovery of the property.

Information to be given at the Metropolitan Police Office, New Scotland Yard, London, S. W., or the Spectacular.

Sir Edward Bradford
Commissioner of Police

Behind the desk, a harried-looking woman strode back and forth, her gloved hands moving restlessly. Cos realised she recognised the lady: it was the Amazing Lumiere's secretary, Miss Fox.

On the other side of the hall, Gustav the Mighty, dressed in his striped leotard, was standing next to the safe that Cos had last seen beneath *The Lady Invalid*. A small gathering looked on.

'I will now demonstrate how easy it is to break into a supposedly unbreakable strongbox,' he announced to his captive audience. The strongman picked up the metal vault as easily as if he were picking up a feather. With an almost lazy flick of his wrist, he lobbed the safe on to the marble floor. The safe rolled, and its doors sprang open with a click. The audience erupted into applause.

'And that *could* be how the thief of *The Lady Invalid* made off with the painting,' Gustav roared over the claps, before taking a bow.

'Cos!' Mary called insistently.

Cos hastened after her friends. She finally saw it: the space where the stolen painting used to be. All that was left was a small metal hook that had secured the painting to the wall. There was nothing else – no frame (that had been found in Cos's father's possession), no smattering of broken glass (that had probably been swept away before visitors were allowed in), no calling card left by the Spectre (Cos supposed that the police had taken that into evidence). The guards had deserted their posts, and even the plush rope barrier had disappeared.

Cos's hope shrivelled away. There were no clues to be found.

Mary blew out a frustrated breath. It seemed she'd come to the same conclusion. But then a curious sound pricked at Cos's ears: a strangled, terrified cry.

Cos strode towards the noise instinctively. A giggling huddle of children stood apart from the crowd, facing something Cos couldn't see. Her eyes narrowed, blood pounding in her ears. All thoughts about the Spectre suddenly vanished. She *had* to help whoever was making that sound. She'd watched the Stain siblings bully and intimidate girls for years, feeling helpless. She refused to stand by and let such cruelty happen any more.

Cos shouldered her way through the group, coming to a halt when she saw a boy lob something towards a snub-nosed cat, which yowled with fear.

Cos's shock mingled with fury as she stepped in between Cat and the children. She bent down to pick up the projectile – a crumpled-up bit of paper.

'Leave her alone,' she said fiercely.

'Is everything all right?' Miss Fox seemed to appear from nowhere as Cos's friends caught up with her. The other children murmured a yes before beating a hasty retreat.

Miss Fox winked at Cos, who grinned gratefully back at her, before the secretary returned to the desk. Cat trilled, and nuzzled her face against Cos's leg.

Cos unfurled the scrunched-up paper. It was an old poster for the New York Spectacular. An idea came to Cos like a lightning bolt.

'Of course!' she muttered. 'Why didn't I see it before? Follow me.' She marched back towards the entrance of the Picture Palace, weaving through the crowd. Her friends followed her, their eyebrows raised, looking confused.

'The last three Spectre thefts,' Cos exclaimed, pointing at the uncovered posters, 'correspond with the last three destinations of the Spectacular! New York, Paris, Berlin. And now London.' She plunged her hands into her pocket, pulling out the jam-splodged *Gazette* where she'd first read about the Spectre. 'See? The thief has to be someone who travelled with the Spectacular!'

Finally, Cos felt a little closer to the truth. At least one of the many mysteries was beginning to make sense: the Spectre was using the Spectacular as cover to commit his crimes.

'That might be why the police are so sure they have the right man,' Miles suggested. 'They can't know that your father has only just been hired as the costumier.'

'Exactly,' Cos muttered.

167

'And it narrows down our suspects by quite a bit,' Mary said. 'A Spectacular employee?'

'Or performer?' added Pearl. 'It *has* to be someone who's been part of the show from the beginning.'

Cos's breath hitched in her throat. 'I bet it's Mr Luminaire. You all heard him – he's blackmailing Sir Vincent *and* he said he couldn't afford any more losses. When *we* were desperate for money, we planned the Treasure Palace Heist. It all fits.'

'His conversation with the art dealer is definitely suspicious,' conceded Mary. 'But we can't jump to conclusions. If we did that, we'd be just as bad as the police.'

'Besides,' Miles said, 'Madame Kaplinsky is equally iffy. She was telling people she could find the missing art.'

'Exactly, Miles,' Mary said. 'We need more than a hunch, Cos – we need evidence. Come on – let's head home and plan our next steps.'

With Mary's warning ringing in Cos's ears, Cos led the way past the fairground wagons and they all headed for home.

CHAPTER EIGHTEEN

As Mary twisted the key in the lock and pushed the front door open, Cos was relieved to see that the entrance foyer looked far tidier: the puddles had been mopped up, the toilet-paper streamers removed from the ceiling and the old records of the Home were piled neatly on the comfy armchair. The other girls had been hard at work.

'ARE YOU HOME?' An excited shout filtered down through the building. 'COME AND SEE WHAT WE'VE DONE!'

Mary groaned. 'If there's more mess upstairs, I might cry.' She sloped towards the rickety staircase, the others following her.

'You coming, Cos?' Diya said, pressing the button to call the lift down to the ground floor.

'I'll be there in a bit,' Cos replied, feeling for the sewing kit in her pocket.

Diya raised an inquisitive eyebrow.

Cos strode towards the schoolroom and their board of investigations. They'd made some progress at the Spectacular, but for Cos it was frustratingly slow. Her father was in a cell somewhere: cold and broken and wrongly accused of being the world's greatest thief.

The injustice of it all rankled. She sat down at a desk, ideas thrumming in her brain, and placed her father's sewing kit on the desk. He had to have given it to her for a reason, and she was determined to figure out what that reason was. She opened it up and spent a few minutes admiring each of the instruments before reading through the other papers her father had tucked inside. The first one she'd glanced at had been ideas for the name of his business, but the others seemed to be tailoring orders.

Instead of being written on prison toilet paper, these orders were scrawled on the back of ripped Spectacular posters and old pieces of paper detailing the Amazing Luminaire's most famous tricks. But all the orders seemed boring and ordinary.

Cos clicked her tongue with frustration. She looked at the teeny thimble – barely the size of her thumb, a small silver cap embossed with tiny stars.

Her tummy lurched.

'Look to the stars,' she muttered to herself. Her mother's saying, and the last thing her father had told her. Could it really be?

She picked up the thimble and turned it over. Her heart leaped. There was something wedged inside. Using her father's tweezers, she carefully prised it free. It was a dog-eared piece of paper, which she placed flat on the desk in front of her.

Cos stretched out her shoulder blades with a satisfying (but painful) click, lit one of Diya's Luminous Lanterns, and stared down at her find.

The piece of paper was ripped at one side, as if it had been torn out of a book, and was the colour of faded parchment. Her father's distinctive letterhead was printed across one side. But this sent a shiver up her spine. There was only one item on the paper, written in Edmund's handwriting:

Starry-night necktie

Cos thought hard. Could that be the necktie that the Spectre had worn whilst fleeing the scene of the crime? The newspaper boy had mentioned it was polka-dotted, but could it instead have been star-dotted?

Her heart sank. Another bit of evidence that suggested a close connection between her father and the Spectre. For a moment, Cos's eyes drifted to the empty schoolroom fireplace. It would only take one lit match to forever destroy the scrap of paper, to erase this link between Edmund Deans and the crimes he'd been accused of. But Cos couldn't do it. The truth mattered, she decided. Even if it was awful.

But as she turned the paper over she frowned. Printed on this side were perfectly drawn squares and rectangles, all pushed together to form one complete shape. Untidy dashes snaked randomly across the squares and rectangles, following a squiggly path that ended in an X.

Cos's heart raced. The last time she'd found something with an X written on it, it had been a map that led to her parents. But this didn't look like any map Cos had ever seen before. For a start, there were no roads or rivers or squares of greenery. That meant that it couldn't possibly be a map of London, like her embroidered map. It seemed too ordered for that.

She stood up, her gaze flickering to their reconstruction of the *Gazette's* investigation into the Spectre. Cos allowed herself to puzzle over *that* mystery for a moment or two before flipping the board over. This side of the blackboard was empty – the perfect blank slate for her tangled ideas.

Cos wrote down on the blackboard every idea that popped into her mind – even the most preposterous ones. Then she went to sit at the desk again, to look at the board and think some more. She tapped the chalk on the desk. Then she stifled a yawn and her eyelids began to flutter closed . . .

CHAPTER NINETEEN

'COS! WHERE ARE YOU?'

Cos woke mid-snore. She was hunched uncomfortably on the desk, the sewing kit poking into her ribs. The schoolroom doors slammed open and Diya rolled in, followed by everyone else.

'Did you fall asleep here?' Diya asked, half disapprovingly and half concerned.

Cos blinked the sleep from her eyes. 'Mmmhmmm.' She suppressed a yawn.

'Guess what I've figured out?' Mary rushed towards Cos, slamming her clipboard on to the desk. 'We've narrowed down the Spectre suspects even more, without trying!' She began to pace in front of the blackboard. 'We know that the Spectre has been using the Spectacular as a front to commit thefts, but that leaves us with a rather large group of people who could potentially be our criminal mastermind. But we can conclusively rule out two of those!'

'Firstly, Madame Kaplinsky can't be the Spectre,' Mary continued. 'Because we saw her at the offices of the *London Gazette* – remember?'

Cos did have a hazy memory of the irate lady shouting as they slipped inside the newspaper building. 'But that doesn't mean she couldn't have stolen the painting,' Cos said. 'It was stolen two days before that.'

'Ah, but she was angry about the *Gazette* reporting that her seance was a hoax! And that seance was held' – Mary paused dramatically to grab a rain-soaked flyer that she had pinned to her clipboard – 'at exactly the time when *The Lady Invalid* disappeared!'

Cos glanced down at the flyer. It read:

THE BRITISH SPIRITUALIST SOCIETY PROUDLY PRESENTS . . .

THE SEANCE-ATHON

Forty-eight hours of talking with the dearly departed, conducted by renowned ghost whisperer Madame Kaplinsky!

Kensington Town Hall.

Commences midnight on 12th March.

'And,' Miles interjected, 'we heard another suspect being ruled out.'

Cos frowned. 'When?'

'At the Spectacular. Mr Luminaire had Sir Vincent tail the Strongman – Gustav the Mighty. It sounded like the illusionist was worried that he might be trying to leave to work with one of the Spectacular's competitors. Sir Vincent found out that Gustav had a secret meeting with the Barnum & Bailey circus – and the meeting was in Dover, so he wasn't even in London when the painting was stolen.'

An excited murmur passed through the other girls, but Cos shook her head. 'But that still leaves us with dozens of other possibilities – the dancers, the fire eaters, the ride operators, even that horrible ticket attendant who wouldn't let us in.'

'Some of those employees might've been hired here in London, like your father, Cos,' suggested Dolly. 'Which means they also can't be the Spectre.'

'But we don't know who they are.' Cos didn't mean to, but she snapped at her friend. 'And the police don't know any of this either, apparently, because otherwise they wouldn't have arrested him!' Cos buried her face in her arms and let sadness engulf her. As she cried, she heard whispers, and gentle footsteps leaving the schoolroom. When she finally looked back up, only Mary, Diya, Pearl, Miles and Dolly remained. Their faces were crinkled with concern.

As Cos tried to find the words to explain how she felt, Mary happened to glance at the blackboard and Cos's messy scribblings. 'What's this?'

'I was trying to understand why my father handed me his sewing kit,' Cos explained, wiping her tears on her sleeve. 'It has to be important, and I think it has something to do with who the Spectre really is.'

'Are you sure he didn't just give it to you to keep it safe for him?' asked Dolly matter-of-factly. 'If he knows who the Spectre is, why didn't he just tell you?'

Cos shrugged. 'I'm not sure. I'm not even sure he knows who it is – but I know he knows *something*, and I know that something is the key to finding the real villain – not ruling out Spectacular employees one by one. We'll be here till Christmas doing that.'

'What's this?' Pearl asked, picking up the order Cos had found hidden in the star-embossed thimble.

'I figured out the message Edmund was trying to give me – look to the stars. He'd hidden an order inside his thimble. But, unfortunately, it points more to his guilt. I think he made the necktie the Spectre was wearing when he stole the paintings.'

Pearl frowned as she turned the paper over and looked at the printed shapes. 'There's something familiar about this . . .' she said.

'I think he wrote his orders down on any bit of paper he could find,' Cos explained. 'But that one *is* the most unusual. At first I thought it was some kind of map, but it doesn't make any sense.'

Mary swiped the paper from Pearl's grasp, turning it over. 'I know what this is,' she said. 'A building plan.'

'A building plan?' Cos repeated, perplexed. 'Why on earth would my father have a building plan?'

'You mentioned Edmund wrote down orders on used bits of paper?' Miles paced back and forth, his eyebrows knitted together in consternation.

Cos nodded. 'Most of them were scraps of paper from the Spectacular, like old posters.'

'And we know that the Spectre is connected to the Spectacular.' A dawning realisation was spreading across Miles's face. 'So what if your dad was asked to make a necktie at the Spectacular, and Edmund scribbled down the order, like always, on a bit of paper he found – but, by accident, that paper was important to the Spectre.'

'But why would a building plan be important?' Cos asked.

'Because it's not *just* a building plan,' Pearl breathed, waving the paper in front of Cos's nose. 'Look at the scribbly lines that lead from the outside into the building, finishing with an X. It looks exactly like the map we created for the Treasure Palace Heist. You were right, Cos: it *is* a map – a map for the Spectre's next target.'

All of a sudden, Cos understood. 'Of course!' She sprang up from the table, ignoring the spiky pain in her legs. 'At first, my father wouldn't have realised its significance – after all, it was just a unremarkable order for a necktie. But when the Spectre was spotted wearing that very necktie when *The Lady Invalid* was stolen, he must've worked out that the building plan was crucial to the Spectre's next crime. His time in prison has made him wary of the police, which is why he didn't report his suspicion.' Cos's heart pounded. 'That's why he was framed – the Spectre was afraid my father was about to unmask him. If only we knew what building he was planning to strike . . .'

'We already do.' Mary grinned. 'We visited it with Miss Meriton. That's the Victoria and Albert Museum.'

'And there's even a time and date!' Miles jabbed towards a faint scribble that hovered above the plan. It read: **Midnight, 15 Mar.**

'That's tonight,' Cos hissed. 'The next Spectre heist is happening tonight at the museum. We have a chance to catch him red-handed and prove my father's innocence.'

Diya's eyebrows were so high they disappeared into her hairline. 'And then what?'

'We don't even know the museum's security arrangements,' Mary said. 'There must be guards, and they'll catch us before we have the chance to catch the Spectre. And we don't even know which item the Spectre is targeting! Less than a day isn't enough time, Cos.'

Cos thought for a beat. 'But everyone thinks the Spectre has already been caught – the guards will be unusually relaxed. And, using this map, we can work out the item he's planning to steal.'

'Cos, this is ridiculous, even for you,' Diya muttered. 'It took us days of hard work to prepare for the Treasure Palace Heist. There's no way we'll be able to do this. And even if we do catch him, do you really think the police will believe you – the daughter of the man they think is the criminal mastermind?'

Cos swallowed. 'I know it's reckless, I do. But I think it might be my – *our* – only chance.' She heard a *click-clack* and turned away, distracted. Pearl had pulled out a ball of violet yarn, and her knitting needles were tapping together as she quickly finished the first row.

'What are you doing, Pearly?' Miles asked.

Pearl shrugged. 'Well, we need something to catch the Spectre in – so I'm knitting us a net.'

Despite herself, Cos grinned. She turned back to Diya and Mary, who had begun to nervously chew on her hair ribbon.

'Come on, Diya,' Cos pleaded. 'You don't want to see another valuable artefact fall into the hands of the Spectre, do you?'

'FINE!' Diya snapped, but her anger was half-hearted. In fact, Cos could see the shadow of an idea flit across her face. 'I will help, on two conditions. Firstly, if the item the Spectre plans to steal belongs to another country, it cannot remain with the museum.'

Cos thought for a moment. She would have to adjust her plan ever so slightly – they could apprehend the Spectre after he'd retrieved the item and take both the thief and his bounty at the same time. 'I can agree to that . . .'

'And secondly,' Diya continued, 'no more going off plan. Mary's nerves are frayed, we're all tired of this gallivanting round London and you're in pain.' Diya narrowed her eyes at Cos. 'I know you think you're disguising it, but we can tell. That's why you fell asleep. Do you promise?' She stuck out her hand.

Cos swallowed. That promise was a little harder to agree to. Grand visions of capturing the Spectre and having a fairytale reunion with her father swam through her mind. And what if they found more clues? How could Cos rest until each and every lead had been chased down?

But she knew her friend was right. A treacherous thought crept into her mind. Although she felt guilty, as she held out one hand to shake Diya's, she crossed the fingers on her other hand.

'I promise,' she croaked.

CHAPTER TWENTY

As evening fell, rain tumbled from the sky above, illuminated in the light given off by the streetlamps. Mary fetched everyone umbrellas (all suitably black, for the occasion of averting a heist), and they went over their plan in the schoolroom one last time.

Cos had only just managed to persuade the other girls to go to bed, even though they were exhausted, having made sure the Home was cleaned to Miss Meriton's standard. They eventually agreed on the condition: cakes for breakfast the next day.

'The Spectre plans to arrive at the museum at midnight sharp,' said Cos softly. The shadows in the schoolroom stretched towards the small pool of light cast by one of Diya's Luminous Lanterns. 'Mary, how are we for time?'

Mary was already jittery about the not-a-heist, even though she had found the museum blueprints *and* identified a way to get into the building unseen. She patted her coat pockets, her face creasing into a frown.

'What is it?' Cos asked.

'My watch,' Mary cried, her eyes welling with tears as she shook out her empty pockets. 'It's not here.'

'Don't worry,' Miles said soothingly. 'When did you last have it?'

Mary's breath came in panicked puffs. 'Er, erm, when we visited the Spectacular the first time.'

Diya frowned. 'That's odd. That's the last time I swear I had my favourite screwdriver.'

Something clicked in Cos's brain. 'And my mum's star.'

'Maybe the painting isn't the only item the Spectre's stolen in London?' Mary asked, her voice wobbling dangerously. She sucked in a calming breath and closed her eyes. When she opened them again, her gaze flicked to the hulking grandfather clock *tick-tocking* next to the coat stand. 'But we should focus on the plan at hand. It's eleven thirty-three exactly, Cos. I've calculated that it'll take us twenty minutes to reach the museum, taking into account your joints.'

'Remember, whilst we don't know the *exact* item the Spectre is targeting,' said Diya, her eyes flashing with determination, 'Mary deduced that the X on the map has to be somewhere in

182

the Indian Museum section. There are lots of stolen treasures there that the Spectre could be after.'

'Great work,' Cos said, turning to Pearl. 'And is your net finished, Pearly?'

The artist nodded, a wry smile crossing her face. 'Diya and I have worked together on a novel way to deploy it.'

'And we're sure that the sewers are the best way to get in?' Miles asked apprehensively.

Mary stepped back to one of the schoolroom desks. Scattered across it were upturned books that ranged in title from *A History of London's Subterranean Tunnels* to *The Kensington Sewer System*. She picked up the bulkiest tome. 'If my research is correct, yes. It's the building's only structural weakness. That way, we'll avoid guards *and* the Spectre.'

Cos tried to nod encouragingly at her friend, despite the fact that she was almost certain that the sewers would contain three of her least favourite things: stairs, bad smells and a yawning darkness.

'Don't worry,' Diya said, sensing Cos's worry immediately. 'I've improved my Rambunctious Ramp to ensure we can get down into the tunnels safely.'

With their plan perfected, they left the Home, slinking in silence into the soggy darkness. Mary led the way, pausing every so often to double-check their route in the glow of her lantern. The evening was busier than Cos had expected:

they weaved between drunken pedestrians and dodged horse-drawn carriages as they walked through Kensington.

Cos's joints groaned under the strain of all this exertion, and she knew it was only a matter of time until the next dislocation occurred.

With Mary's expert directions, soon they found themselves looking up at an unimpressive patchwork of buildings marred by scaffold skeletons. The Victoria and Albert Museum was in the middle of renovations, with brand-new buildings being constructed to house the treasures inside.

Mary led them past the museum's entrance, and they dashed round the corner to Exhibition Road. To Cos's relief, the road was deserted.

Mary scurried towards a circular cover embedded in the centre of the road. Miles knelt down and began to prise it loose. Pearl held her lantern so they could see, and Diya busied herself with hoisting the new, improved Rambunctious Ramp from the handles of her wheelchair. As soon as Mary had mentioned the sewer system in her *PLAN TO BREAK INTO THE MUSEUM*, Diya retreated to her invention station, a familiar spark in her eyes.

Diya shook the ramp, and with a *whoosh* it expanded. It was now ladder-length – far longer than the prototype Diya had debuted at the Spectacular. Cos was speechless. Sometimes words weren't enough to describe Diya's brilliance. Cos could immediately see that the ramp would create a kind of slope into the tunnel, allowing Diya to wheel safely down.

'I know stairs can be a little tricky for you, Cos, so I adapted my wheelchair so you can use the ramp too.' Diya shoved aside the bags that covered the back of her chair, revealing a small platform just behind the rear wheels. Cos then noticed a hook attached to the handle of Diya's chair.

A smile grew wide across Cos's face. 'Is that . . .?'

'It's a stand for you, and a walking stick-rest,' Diya said. 'So we can slide down together.'

Cos didn't know what to say. Instead she limped forward and gave Diya the biggest hug possible.

Miles and Mary heaved the heavy metal circle upwards, and it opened with a cavernous yawn. Cos peered down the hole into a vast and unblinking darkness. She could just about make out a ladder that disappeared into the tunnel.

Pearl went first. 'For Cos's father, Aggie and Miss Meriton,' she said, in the way that adults did when they raised their wine glasses for a toast.

'For Cos's father, Aggie and Miss Meriton,' the others repeated. Their toast reverberated into the tunnel, sending ghostly echoes ricocheting back.

With their lanterns slicing beams of light through the inky black, Pearl, Mary and Miles descended. After what seemed like forever, distant splashes told Cos and Diya that they'd reached the bottom of the ladder.

'We're all right. The water is much shallower than I expected.' Mary's whisper echoed up to the surface. 'Diya – deploy the ramp.'

Back at ground level, Cos and Diya slid the ramp on to the topmost step, threading the other end down into the darkness. With a metallic clank, the end hit the floor. There were a couple of jolts as their friends adjusted it, and then a whisper. 'Ready when you are.'

Diya lined up her wheelchair at the mouth of the hole, her wheels just touching the metal of the ramp. Then she put her brakes on. Cos stepped on to the platform that had been made for her, slotting her walking stick into its rest. Then she took a firm grip of Diya's handles, gritted her teeth and looked up at the twinkling stars above, remembering her mother's saying: *Keep your feet on the ground, but always remember to look to the stars.*

'Ready?' Diya whispered.

'Yes,' Cos breathed.

'Hold on tiggghhhhhhht.'

Even though Cos knew what was coming, it was still a shock. It started off slowly, with Diya's wheelchair wobbling on the precipice – before it hurtled down.

The wind whooshed past Cos's head. Her hair whipped around, obscuring her vision, but she caught glimpses of crescent-shaped brick tunnels, a trickling stream and the

rapidly approaching figures of her three friends. With an almighty splash, Diya's wheelchair hit the two inches of water in the sewer, sending a tidal wave hurtling towards Pearl, Miles and Mary, who were waiting at the far end of the tunnel. The water slowed them slightly, as Diya struggled to gain control of her chair. The wheels squeaked as she squeezed the brakes, and the wheelchair teetered violently, threatening to spill Cos and Diya into the watery tunnel.

There was one final teeter, and Diya's Luminous Lantern fell from her lap, smashing into a thousand shards of glass and plunging them into almost darkness.

Cos stumbled off the platform, leaning on her walking stick. Breathing heavily, she fell into Mary's arms.

'It's all right,' Mary whispered, patting Cos on the head.

'It's MORE than all right!' Cos replied, her voice echoey in the unfamiliar gloom of the tunnel. 'That was incredible, exhilarating! I want to do it again! It was a thousand times better than the rides at the Spectacular fairground.' Cos felt like whooping. Goose pimples rushed up her arm as she let out her breath, a sense of sheer *aliveness* shivering through her.

Miles hurried back up the ladder, pulling the circular cover back in place and sliding the ramp from the topmost rung. As he climbed back down, the metal slats slid together, and by the time he reached the bottom Diya's Rambunctious Ramp was its original size again. With a satisfied smirk, Diya hooked it on to the back of her wheelchair.

A curved stone tunnel stretched ahead, a trickling stream of dubious cleanliness surging by their feet – and wheels. Cos splashed forward in her effort to keep up with the others.

'Aha, this is it!' Mary's light licked up the red bricks, illuminating a sign that read **MUSEUM OUTLET**.

A ladder disappeared into the darkness above. Miles twirled out his lock-picking kit and scampered up the ladder. The *clink-clank-clunks* from above told Cos that he was trying to prise the manhole cap free. Whilst he did that, Mary pulled the Rambunctious Ramp from the handles of Diya's chair, and Pearl retrieved one of Diya's older inventions – the Wondrous Winch – from a tool bag. She attached the winch to the front of Diya's chair with a metal hook and tucked the hand crank under her arm. Then Mary and Pearl took one corner of the ramp each and began to climb. The ramp extended and the Wondrous Winch's spool of rope unfurled with every step.

When the girls reached the top of the ladder, they'd created a steep metal slide and a slack rope connecting the tunnel to the surface. Cos stepped back on the platform Diya had installed for her.

'One,' Mary said, her voice echoing. 'Two . . . three! Heave!'

The rope went taut. As Mary and Pearl pulled, Diya furiously pumped her arms, spinning her wheels round and round. The wheelchair travelled up the ramp in fits and starts. Just as they reached the mouth of the manhole, hands reached out, grabbing Diya's wheelchair, and Diya and Cos were heaved over the threshold.

CHAPTER TWENTY-ONE

'Brilliant,' whispered Mary as she consulted her plan by lantern light after they'd peeked out of the cupboard into which they'd emerged. 'I think we're right by the Indian Museum in the Eastern Galleries.'

Cos cast her mind back to their visit to the museum with Miss Meriton, wishing she'd paid more attention. 'What does the museum contain?'

'Lots of artefacts from India,' Mary replied. 'All were taken by the East India Company, which donated its collection. There are nine whole rooms full of objects.'

Beside Cos, Diya let out a world-weary sigh. 'Of course they didn't just . . . I don't know . . . take it all back to India.'

Cos gave her friend a fierce squeeze. Diya was rightfully proud of her Indian heritage – and rightfully furious about her

190

country's mistreatment at the hands of the British Empire.

The museum at night sent shivers running up Cos's spine. Their lanterns didn't chase away nearly enough shadows. Mary was relatively certain that the museum's watchmen only patrolled the central galleries, but they'd agreed that too much light would attract unwanted attention, particularly if the Spectre would also soon be stalking the corridors.

Mary led the others towards a small sign above the archway that read *INDIAN MUSEUM*. When Mary's lantern lit up the walls of the room beyond, Cos caught glimpses of fearsomely sharp spears and swords, and an ornately embellished fringed canopy that hung over a delicate golden box. As she stepped over the threshold, Cos spun round, holding her lantern high to illuminate the many display cases filled with ancient earthenware, engraved stone tablets and silver medallions. This first room had three further archways, leading to even more wonder-filled galleries.

'Right,' Mary whispered, nose buried in her map. 'I can't pinpoint exactly the item the X marks, so we need to search each room. Keep a lookout for one-of-a-kind items – those are the usual targets. And flash your lantern if you find anything.' With a business-like nod, Mary stalked off, followed by Pearl. Miles and Cos took the left archway, and Diya wheeled to the right.

Cos soon realised she was more than out of her depth.

Every artefact she peered at seemed to her to be uniquely beautiful and unlike anything she'd seen before. From the silk saris to the woven grass mats, Cos was overwhelmed by the richness and splendour of the Indian Museum, and how out of place it was encased in rainy, cold England. Miles's bewildered expression told her he was thinking the same.

Before she could suggest that they see how the others were getting on, there was a deliberate series of flashes:

.._. ___ .._ _. _.. /.._

Or, in Morse code: *FOUND IT.*

Cos and Miles paused only to exchange a glance before barrelling in the direction of the message. They all gathered in the furthest room of the Indian Museum. Diya stared reverently at a display case atop a handsome mahogany stand in the centre of the room. As Cos drew near, she held her lantern up, throwing light on the artefact perched on a plush velvet cushion in the cabinet.

'What is *that*?' Pearl whispered.

'*That* is the Siraj elephant,' Diya explained. 'It's a famous mechanical toy – an automaton that moves and makes sounds when it is wound up. It was made for Siraj ud-Daulah, the ruler of Bengal, in the eighteenth century. When the British defeated and executed the Siraj ud-Daulah and his family, his elephant was stolen and taken to Britain. It's a very beautiful item – made of gold and embossed with all sorts of gems. And it's one of a kind. The perfect Spectre target.'

Cos drew nearer to get a better look. The Siraj elephant was small enough to fit in the palm of her hand. It was made of golden cogs and studded with rubies and emeralds, its tail in the shape of a key.

'That's how it winds up,' whispered Diya. 'And then the elephant can walk about. It's really quite a remarkable mechanical.'

'It's beautiful,' Cos breathed.

'If you're sure this is what he's after, then we need to hide,' Mary warned. 'The Spectre could be here at any moment.' She glanced around the shadowy gallery. 'How about behind those?' She pointed to a pair of heavy embroidered tapestries that hung on the walls. 'It isn't an ideal hiding place, but it will do.'

'Once we extinguish our lanterns, it'll be so dark I don't think the Spectre will spot the lumps my wheelchair will make. Here, Cos,' Diya said, taking a familiar contraption from her wheelchair bag and handing it to her. Cos noticed that it had been altered since the last time they'd used it, and now had Pearl's newly knitted net attached to its metal nozzle.

'Do you remember my Great Grabber?' Diya asked.

Cos did, vividly. She'd been seconds from plummeting out

of the dormitory window last year when Diya's grappling hook had snatched her from the air and pulled her safely inside.

'Well, with a bit of tinkering, and Pearl's excellent net-making, it's been repurposed. It's now called the Spectre Snarer. When you press this lever' – Diya pointed towards a small trigger atop the nozzle – 'the Snarer will propel Pearl's net forward with such ferocity that not only will the Spectre be completely bamboozled, but he won't know he's trapped till it's too late.'

'Diya,' Cos exclaimed, a little louder than she intended. 'I know I say this a lot, but you are a GENIUS!'

Even in the darkened museum, Cos thought she saw her friend blush.

'But you have to be careful with it,' Diya continued. 'We've only got one shot, and it has to be timed perfectly.'

Cos nodded, thinking everything over. 'We need to trap the Spectre, but we also want to steal the elephant, so it can go back to its rightful home in India. So I think we'll have to wait until he's actually got it out of the display case, then act before he makes his escape. I think there's only one person here who can be relied upon to get those calculations correct.'

She turned to Mary.

'Me? Cos, no. I can't.' Mary backed away from the Spectre Snarer as though it were a dangerous explosive. 'What if I ruin everything? Or tremble so much that the net misses the

Spectre?' Her eyes filled with tears. 'Please don't make me.'

Cos frowned. 'I'd never make you do something you didn't want to do, M. All right, let's think of a compromise. I'll fire the Snarer, but Mary will tell me when. Diya, your wheelchair will require a little more tapestry to hide it, so why don't you and Miles conceal yourselves over there, and us three will hide here?' She pointed to the hanging tapestry closest to the elephant's display case.

They all rushed into position. Crouching behind the tapestry, Cos peeked between the feathers that bedecked its edge. The feathers tickled her skin, and from the wriggling at the other end of the tapestry, it seemed that Pearl felt it as well. The darkness was all encompassing. All Cos could hear was the familiar *thud-thud-thud* of her heartbeat. She shifted the Snarer on to her shoulder, and hoped the Spectre would hurry up.

A prickle of light piercing the darkness alerted Cos to the master thief's presence. Cos sucked in a breath as a black-cloaked figure crept towards the display case. He held a torch, which he balanced on top of the glass cabinet, allowing Cos to see the gallery in shades of grey.

A tingle crept up Cos's spine. *The Spectre.*

The Spectre placed a leather bag on the floor, then took out a pointed tool that glinted in the torchlight. In one fluid movement, he cut a perfect circle in the glass of the display case. Cos gaped as the thief placed a gloved finger in the centre of the circle, tipping back the glass and pulling it free. He placed the glass circle carefully on the floor and went to reach for the elephant.

Mary nudged Cos. The tapestry fluttered. The girls pressed themselves flat against the wall as the Spectre turned towards the sound.

Silence. Cos counted out three seconds before the Spectre turned back round, his fingers outstretched towards the elephant.

Anticipation buzzed through her. This was it – their chance to find out who the Spectre really was. She narrowed her eyes, zeroing in on every little thing about the strange figure.

Heavy velvet cloak in midnight black.

Smart leather loafers with gold buckles.

Hunched shoulders, short stature.

At Cos's side, Mary held up three fingers.

Cos's gaze was trained on the Spectre as he plucked the Siraj elephant from its cushion and began to carefully thread it through the hole he'd cut in its case.

Mary put one finger down.

Cos pointed the Snarer squarely at the thief.

Mary curled down another finger as the Spectre clasped the elephant to his chest.

Cos's finger hovered above the Spectre Snarer's trigger. She leaned forward, her nose brushing up against one of the many feathers. She took an unexpected breath in as she pressed down on the lever, and—

'Achooooo!'

Cos's sneeze splintered the silence . . . and the net she'd fired flew hopelessly wide.

The figure whirled round, but his hood fell so low that most of his face was shadowed. For a beat, the figure froze, then he picked up his torch and bag, shoved the stolen elephant inside it, then upended the empty display case. The case fell to the floor and shattered.

Then the Spectre scarpered, charging past them, his cloak billowing behind. As Cos and Mary fought to untangle themselves from the tapestry, Miles and Pearl were hot on the villain's tail, leaping over the broken glass in hot pursuit. Diya reversed her chair from her hiding place, manoeuvring towards the Spectre. Mary followed and Cos – as usual – brought up the rear, puffing as she struggled to keep up with Diya's chair.

'Cos, Diya – head left!' Mary hissed as they dived into the Indian Glassware Room, dodging ancient jars and intricately painted bottles.

'What?' Cos frowned. 'The Spectre's going straight ahead.'

'Just trust me!' Mary insisted.

Dutifully, Cos and Diya turned into a corridor lined with display glasses. *Ah*, Cos realised, *a shortcut.*

'Right,' whispered Mary when they'd reached the end of the hall, 'then right again.'

As Mary sprinted back on to the main concourse of the Indian Museum, she collided with the Spectre. Mary screeched and fell to the floor, but the Spectre stayed upright and continued running. As Miles and Diya reached the trembling Mary, Pearl leaped over her, still following the Spectre.

'Are you all right, Mary?' Cos asked her friend, who was curled up in a ball, shivering.

Mary uncurled. Cradled in her hand was the tiny elephant automaton. 'I managed to swipe it from him,' she whispered.

Before they could celebrate that at least one part of their not-a-heist had gone to plan, there was a huge crash.

'Pearl!' squeaked Mary, handing the Siraj elephant to Diya for safe-keeping. She pushed herself to standing and ran in the direction of the sound, followed swiftly by Miles. When Cos caught up, she realised what had happened. The Spectre had smashed through a side door to escape the museum. Pearl was crouched there, surrounded by broken glass.

'We lost him,' huffed Miles.

'We couldn't have done anything else,' Cos said, but she felt as feeble as a newly hatched butterfly. That had been their best – no, their only – chance to pin down the Spectre.

But they had been outsmarted. There was a sharp pain in her side; she wasn't sure whether that was down to her crushing disappointment or the unexpected running. 'I'm so sorry I ruined everything.'

'We didn't lose him,' Pearl said, uncurling herself. She raised a shaking hand and pointed at a curious line of sand that led away from the smashed glass of the door. With her other hand, she took out what looked like a glass beaker filled with sand, its neck narrow. On its back was a small metal clip. 'I managed to attach one of these to the Spectre's cloak.'

'What is it?' Mary asked.

Pearl grinned. 'I thought about how useful it would be if we could track the Spectre – like a dog does with a scent. Then I took inspiration from Diya and invented a tracker.'

A wide smile cracked Diya's face. 'I don't think I've ever been called an inspiration before. Thank you, Pearly! So how does it work?'

Pearl grinned back, holding up her creation. 'It's one half of an hourglass. An hourglass works by letting small increments of sand out, bit by bit. So I halved one, and used some glue to attach a clip to the back.'

Cos's mouth fell open.

Diya wheeled herself over to get a better look at Pearl's first invention. 'What are you going to name it?'

Pearl blushed a deep crimson. 'The Tremendous Tracker.'

'This is going to lead us straight to the Spectre?' wheezed Miles, still a little winded from his run.

Pearl nodded. In the distance, there were shouts and the thuds of footsteps. *Security.*

'We need to get out of here,' Cos said, nodding towards the Spectre-shaped hole in the smashed door. 'Let's follow him.'

CHAPTER TWENTY-TWO

They followed the twists and turns of Pearl's sand trail down the street, using the gaslights to see their way. Cos gritted her teeth with every step. Her joints ached something chronic, but she pushed on – for her father. Yet by the time the sand trail rounded the street corner, the shine of their pursuit had somewhat worn off. Drizzle had scuffed the sand, creating gaps in their route, but even in the damp and the darkness they just about managed to keep track of Pearl's clever tracker.

They weaved through streets, passing packed pubs and dodging drunks on their way home. Soon the map of Kensington Cos held in her head faded, and even Mary seemed a little lost. The cartographer's eyebrows were knitted together, and she was furiously scribbling down street names and landmarks she recognised on the paper attached to her clipboard.

'Where *are* we going?' Mary asked as the trail careened to the left, into an alley.

'Wherever it is, I hope we get there soon,' grumbled Cos, rubbing her knee. She was so focused on each painful step that she bumped into Miles. 'Why did you stop?' she asked, not entirely un-grumpily.

Miles didn't answer. He was staring up at a monstrosity of a building ahead of them, half hidden behind an iron fence. It was a half-built white marble mansion, the size of which Cos had never seen, with symmetrical turrets stretching skywards, creating an almost royal feel. A huge mound of earth sat in front of the house, a hulking steel crane next to it, and wooden scaffolding clung to one wing.

The sand trail snaked through the chained, padlocked gates that led to the unfinished mansion. The Spectre had sneaked inside. But why?

As Cos stepped forward and gave the padlock a good shake (it was, most definitely, securely bolted), she realised that Miles was still frozen, staring open-mouthed at the building.

'Miles.' Cos grabbed his hand. 'Are you all right?'

Miles blinked and shook his head. 'It's just, er, I know this place. It used to be the Rookery.'

'The what?'

Miles let out a deep breath, kicking at some rubble at the edge of the fence. 'The Rookery was a slum. Thousands of people were crammed into a handful of falling-down houses. They dressed in rags, and most didn't even wear shoes. Many fell into crime, because it was the only way to survive.'

A shiver crawled between Cos's shoulder blades and stayed there.

'But it's good, isn't it?' Mary said in a small voice. 'That the Rookery isn't here any more, that those people don't have to live in such horrible conditions any longer?'

Miles swallowed, shaking his head. 'Where did those people go, though, M? The Rookery might have been awful, but it was home. And now it's all been torn down to make way for just one colossal house. I bet whoever built that–' he nodded towards the mansion, '– doesn't care. And the people who were cleared out are probably even worse off now . . .'

A horrible silence stretched between the friends. Miles took out his lock-picking kit and began to work on the padlock. 'Aha,' he said flatly as it clicked open, the heavy chains sliding to the ground. 'After you.'

As they cautiously tiptoed into the grounds of the mysterious mansion, Cos realised two things: firstly, this house was even grander than she'd thought. It even had a glistening lake, its water reflecting the stars above. Stone pathways weaved around a landscaped garden where topiary was shaped into impossible creatures and flowers the colours of jewels bloomed.

Secondly, it was less than half finished. Sculptures had been left half carved, wheelbarrows full of weeds were dotted about the garden and mounds of earth littered the landscape. Pearl led the way as they traipsed over the manicured lawn towards an imposing arched door that was set in the centre of the white building. But as Miles knelt down to pick the lock it swung open.

They stole inside. The entrance hall was cavernous and paved in a marble that gleamed under the light of their lanterns. A huge central staircase led to the first floor, the end of its handrails carved into gargoyles.

'Whoa,' muttered Miles, holding his lantern closer to examine them.

Whoa, whoa, whoa, whoa, echoed back at them.

Other than the staircase, the entrance hall was empty. There was no furniture, no frames adorning the walls, nothing. *It feels,* Cos thought, *like a house devoid of everything that makes a building a home.*

Their footsteps echoed as they walked through the mansion, peering into each room as they crept past. Each one was exactly like the entrance hall: pristine, but empty. The nervous knot in Cos's stomach got tighter.

'I've never seen a building so . . . brand-new before,' Pearl whispered, wrinkling her nose at the smell of fresh paint. 'It's odd.'

'Very odd. But whose house is it?' asked Cos. 'And why did the Spectre come *here*, of all places?'

As they peered out into the walled courtyard at the centre of the mansion, they saw a crooked, falling-down building, completely at odds with the newness that surrounded it.

'That's a Rookery house,' Miles exclaimed, almost excitedly, running towards it.

The drizzle had now turned into rain, leaving the courtyard cobbles slick and slippery. Weeds poked between the stones. The building itself was little more than a one-storey outhouse, and looked so ramshackle that Cos wouldn't have been surprised if a strong gust of wind had brought it down. It was one step away from a ruin.

'So the builder of this grand house decided not to demolish one shed?' Diya asked, looking confused. 'Why?'

'This isn't a shed,' Miles said, his eyes sad, pushing open the wonky door. 'This is a house. At least one family – probably more – lived here.'

Cos peered over Miles's shoulder into the shadowy room. There was no floor, just dirt on the ground. A bucket and broomstick sat in one corner, rainwater dripping into the bucket from a hole in the roof. A fuzzy black mould crept up the cracked walls.

Cos's Luminous Lantern chased away some of the shadows as she stepped across the threshold, followed by her friends.

The lantern illuminated the shack. Cos gripped her walking stick and tiptoed further into the building.

There was a single wooden chair and a small table covered in broken gin bottles. Slung on the chair were a heavy black cloak and a pair of gold-buckled loafers – the Spectre's disguise from the museum! – along with a crumpled star-dotted necktie . . . and Pearl's magnificent tracker. The artist carefully unclipped her creation from the hem of the cloak as Cos stepped further into the gloom – and gasped.

In one corner was a pile of treasure, like a dragon's hoard. There were jewelled brooches, pearl-drop earrings, reading monocles and velvet purses. Cos ran a hand over the jumble of items, and her fingers curled round something she recognised – not because she'd ever seen it before, but because she'd read about it. *A diamond necklace*. Cos's heart thumped. She rummaged through the pile a little longer, desperately searching for her star clip, but it wasn't there. Instead she found a gilded violin case and a ticking pocket watch.

Marie Antoinette's necklace, vanished from a Paris museum.

A timepiece, taken from a ball in New York.

In Berlin, a priceless violin stolen.

And that was just the last three thefts – here there were also glittering tiaras, exotic vases and gold aplenty.

'The Spectre's stolen items,' exclaimed Mary.

Behind Cos, Pearl gasped. Cos turned to see her lifting

some of the broken glass from the table, revealing an age-yellowed piece of paper with a very familiar letterhead:

THE HOME FOR UNFORTUNATE GIRLS
NORTH END ROAD, KENSINGTON

Kensington
1st June 1886

Dear Miss Reynard,

I am sorry to hear that you are unable to care for your child and have decided to relinquish custody of her to our institution. The staff here have vast experience in the rearing of defectives, and whilst your child is condemned to remain a hopeless cripple I can assure you she will be treated appropriately.

Yours sincerely,
Miss Whymper (Matron of the Home for Unfortunate Girls)

'Whoever lived here was one of us!' Mary exclaimed as she peered at the letter. 'I remember the name Whymper cropping up when the builders unearthed those old records. She was the matron before the Stains.'

'You don't think the Spectre built this, do you?' Miles said suddenly, his eyes lighting up as he waved at the half-finished mansion. 'Using the money from some of the thefts? They tore down most of the Rookery, but they couldn't bring themselves to destroy this house because . . . because it was once home?'

Cos's heart thumped. The thought that the Spectre could once have been a Home child felt wrong somehow. Nobody who was one of them would want to wreak the kind of havoc that the Spectre had. No, she decided firmly. There had to be some other explanation. Children like her didn't grow up to be villains.

Diya peeled another paper off the table; it was bordered in black and sent a chill through Cos.

KENSINGTON POOR UNION PAUPER'S FUNERAL

MISS SUSANNAH REYNARD

DIED 28th DECEMBER 1886, AGED 28 YEARS

Interred in communal unmarked grave

'She died,' Diya said softly. 'Only a few months after her child went to the Home.'

'What's a *poor-per*?' Pearl asked.

'Paupers' funerals are what happens when you die poor. It happens all the time in the workhouse – lots of people are buried together, in one grave, and none of them have a headstone.' Mary's face blanched. Cos knew she was thinking of her grandpa.

A horrid feeling clawed its way up Cos's throat. Whoever had lived in this rundown house had had a disabled child. She'd died – just after Christmas – after sending her child to live at the Home in which Cos now lived. It had happened nearly fifteen years ago, but the similarities between her life and this child's life were startling. Two disabled children, two dead mothers, two . . . thieves? Bile rose in Cos's throat. A few days ago, she'd been full of admiration for the Spectre's incredible crime spree. But her admiration had crumbled, just like this Rookery house. Stealing back the already stolen was one thing, but stealing with such unrestrained greed was horrid.

'What do we do with this?' Diya was saying, pointing at the hoard. 'The police are hardly likely to believe us if we tell them the Spectre's stolen items are hidden in a slum house concealed behind a newly built mansion. Plus, if we take any of the stolen items to the police, they'll just say that Cos's dad had them all along.'

'And,' said Pearl, 'none of these items were stolen from the Spectacular in London. The Spectre has been thieving for years. The missing painting is nowhere to be seen.'

Miles narrowed his eyes. 'I bet the Spectre's got some sort of lock-up at the fair itself, and they only transfer the stolen goods just before the Spectacular travels to its next destination.'

'Which it's doing after the Midnight Masquerade on Friday,' added Mary breathlessly. 'We need to come up with a plan – the Masquerade might be our last hope to catch the Spectre red-handed.'

Cos's gaze had snagged on a familiar item, hanging neatly on the back of the door of the shack. *A red velvet suit and diamanté bow tie.* She marched over, pressing her nose to it and inhaling the ghost of the smell of mint sprigs and coffee. *Father.*

'This costume belongs to Mr Luminaire!' Cos said. 'He must be the Spectre. He's used the Spectacular as a front for his crimes, and he framed my father. He is the perfect suspect – we should go straight to the police.'

Her friends looked uneasy.

'But, Cos,' Diya said gently, 'Mr Luminaire gave that bow tie to your father to fix. The police would just think that Edmund left it here.'

A frustrated groan escaped Cos's throat. Why was everything so difficult?

'P-p-plus, if Miles is right and the Spectre grew up here, then she's a girl!' Mary stammered.

Cos shook her head, even as Mary's words rattled around her brain. 'You're wrong,' she snapped, angry tears welling in her eyes. 'No one who'd lived at the Home would ever grow up to be this . . . needlessly cruel. Stealing for stealing's sake.

210

Framing an innocent man.' She stared at her friends, daring them to challenge her.

'But, Cos,' Pearl said, in barely more than a whisper, 'we stole. Maybe not needlessly. And *you* admired the Spectre and their impossible heists.'

'I'm nothing like that criminal,' Cos spat, clutching the bow tie. 'You can stay here and think all you want, but I'm going to actually do something. I'm going to give the police concrete proof that he's the thief – proof even they can't ignore.'

And, with that, Cos stalked from the courtyard and slammed the door behind her.

CHAPTER TWENTY-THREE

The building loomed tall and monstrous above Cos, casting shadows across the street. She had drifted through the streets of Kensington, sniffing back tears and clinging to the (by now) very damp bow tie as the sky faded from inky black to a dull grey. Morning had arrived. She stumbled towards the door of the West London Magistrates Court and Police Station, fear in her heart.

At the opposite side of the lobby, a dour-faced man hunched over a small wooden desk. On either side of him was a hulking door. One, Cos deduced, must lead to the cells where her father had been held. The other door, Cos decided, must lead to the offices of the detective that had arrested her father. She tried to push down her rage at the injustice of it all as she strode towards the desk.

The man at the desk glared at her as she reached him.

'Good morning,' Cos said. 'I need to see Detective Constable Wensleydale immediately. I have important evidence in the Spectre case.' She readied herself for an argument, and possibly for a break-in to the police officer's quarters. Without Miles's expert lock-picking, it would be tricky, but Cos was determined that she would not take no for an answer. But to Cos's surprise the man simply shrugged and slipped from his desk, holding a jangling ring of keys. Selecting the oldest-looking, most rusty key, he inserted it into the lock then pushed open the door.

Cos nodded her thanks then stepped inside. The door closed behind her and she tiptoed on, the bow tie crumpled in her hands. The entire office had gathered at the desk at the furthest end of the room. Men – some dressed in the familiar navy uniform, and others in smart shirts and slacks – surrounded someone.

The air was thick with tobacco smoke that clogged Cos's throat. Raucous laughter drifted towards her, and she caught snippets of conversation.

'Knew it from the outset, of course,' growled a gruff voice that Cos had heard before. 'It's my detective instincts, you see – can't be taught. I had my man – the Spectre. A journalist from the *Gazette* is stopping by this afternoon – they want to interview me as the hero who brought down a worldwide criminal.'

There was a chorus of appreciative grunts. Cos paused behind the desk, and, one by one, the men spotted her. Ten stern, moustachioed faces stared at her, and the man she'd come to see – Detective Constable Wensleydale – leaned back in his chair so far that he was almost lying down, his feet up on his empty desk.

There was no flicker of recognition in his eyes. Cos was used to this. A lot of people seemed to forget children like her and her friends almost the moment they set eyes on them. But, when his gaze fell to her walking stick, he frowned.

'Off you go, boys,' he said, dismissing the other men with a wave of his hand. They drifted away, some heading to surrounding desks, and others gathering handcuffs and helmets before heading out on patrol. As soon as they were out of earshot, Detective Constable Wensleydale stood up.

'What do you want?' he asked, scowling. 'I'm guessing you're from that *Home*,' he added, as though Cos had crawled out of a puddle and slithered into his office.

'You've got the wrong man,' Cos said, her voice coming out slightly more squeaky and mouselike than she intended. 'And I can prove it.'

'Leave the investigating to grown-ups, girl.' Wensleydale shook his head. 'And don't repeat that accusation. The Spectre has been caught. That's the end of it.' He turned away from her and sat back down at his desk.

Cos spluttered. That *couldn't* be the end of it. She wouldn't let it. She brandished the crumpled bow tie at him. 'This is the bow tie that the Amazing Luminaire wears when he's performing. I found it, along with some of the items stolen by the Spectre, in a half-built mansion a few streets away. I can show you where if you—'

'Look,' drawled Wensleydale, fiddling with the golden cufflinks at his wrist, 'the case is closed. That's the end of the matter.'

He gathered up the mess on his desk before turning from her and stalking away, and Cos spotted something he missed that made her gasp. A piece of paper had fluttered to the floor. Cos bent down to pick it up. It was a tiny calling card, with barely legible handwriting scrawled across it:

The Spectre

Cos's blood ran cold. She had seen that handwriting before. She knew who it belonged to. How could she have missed something so obvious? She'd read all about the mastermind's infamous calling card, left at every crime scene, but she'd never seen it before.

Her heart pounding, Cos staggered out of the building, taking the calling card with her.

CHAPTER TWENTY-FOUR

As Cos drifted back to the Home, the puzzle pieces of the mystery of the Spectre were finally clicking into place. She'd first seen that handwriting when they'd sneaked into the Spectacular and happened to end up in the records wagon. She'd seen it again on the threat they'd found hidden in Aggie's desk. She'd seen it for the third time on an order for Edmund's business, tucked neatly into his sewing kit. That was why he'd been so keen to give it to her – maybe her father didn't know who exactly the Spectre was, but he knew it was a clue.

Miss Fox was the Spectre.

Cos's thoughts were scrambled. It was unthinkable that the kindly, meek secretary could secretly be a criminal mastermind, but Cos knew that appearances could be deceiving. After all, no one had suspected her and her friends of the Treasure Palace Heist.

Cos realised they were running out of time: it was the Spectacular's last night in London, the date of the Midnight Masquerade. By tomorrow, the Spectre and all evidence of her crimes would be gone. They had only hours to clear her father's name – *and* find Miss Meriton and Aggie.

And, as far as Cos knew, none of her friends were currently talking to her. Which was understandable, Cos thought guiltily. She had been so rude, so dismissive of their thoughts. She had been so wrapped up in her battle to prove her father's innocence that she hadn't considered that her friends were hurting as well. They'd lost their matron, and Aggie. Cos *had* to make it right. She realised that she couldn't do it all by herself – they had to work together if they were going to bring the Spectre down.

Cos gritted her teeth, pushing herself to walk as fast as the pain allowed, running through a newly forming plan, and her apologies, in her head.

The plan was even more ridiculous, even more far-fetched, than her idea to steal five priceless jewels from the Empire Exhibition. In fact, Cos thought it was almost impossible. She knew she'd have a mountain to climb to persuade the girls and Miles to agree to her reckless idea.

When she burst into the entrance foyer of the Star

217

Diamond Home, a most unexpected sight startled her into a frozen silence. A wave of noise hit Cos – chatter, laughter and singing. None of her friends seemed to have noticed her slip through the front door.

The recently tidied Home was tidy no longer. But, unlike the other day, this mess seemed far more purposeful. The Home had been transformed into a sort of workroom. A clothes rack next to the rickety stairs was stuffed with half-finished costumes, and swathes of fabric were strewn across the floor and draped over the comfy armchair. Pearl wore a measuring tape like a scarf round her neck, and she had pins clamped between her lips as she encased Diya's wheelchair in a shimmering material. Diya wasn't paying any attention to Pearl's pinning – she was too busy using a pair of pliers to fiddle with a complicated-looking canister. Her silent fireworks!

Standing next to Pearl, Miles was puzzling at a pair of silver glinting handcuffs locked round his wrists. He wiggled his fingers, twisting his arms this way and that. He spun round – a blur of boy and handcuffs. When he came to a stop, Cos's jaw dropped. The previously secured cuffs were now dangling from Miles's finger, and a triumphant grin played across his face.

'Bravo, Miles!' Mary exclaimed as she shuffled a stack of paper. She was sitting at a schoolroom desk that had been pulled into the foyer, filing documents into a folder that was marked *EVIDENCE THAT EDMUND DEANS IS **NOT** THE SPECTRE.*

On the opposite side of the foyer, the other girls were helping each other pull on garments, eyebrows knitted together in concentration as they sewed hems, tucked in blouses and cut up material. Dolly was midway through stitching tiger stripes on to a top, Ida stuck out her tongue as she carefully painted a thin metal tube mahogany-brown and Ottilie was putting the final touches to a rather fetching shark hat. Maud was carefully taping a small brown package. Cos noticed that written shakily across the package was the address: *The Indian National Association, Calcutta, India.*

Cos stared at them, open-mouthed, all thoughts of plans and shenanigans gone.

Miles spotted her. 'Look who's back!'

The chatter faded.

'What are you doing?' Cos croaked.

'Isn't it obvious?' Diya replied drily. 'The Midnight Masquerade is this evening, the Spectre is still free and the painting is still missing. We're going to break into the Spectacular and steal it back, just as you're plotting to do. But we're going to do it together.'

'All of us,' Dolly added brightly.

Tears pricked at Cos's eyes. *I don't have time for crying,* she told herself sternly. 'How did you know what I was planning?'

'Because we know you, Cos,' Mary said.

'It's that chaos in your eyes,' Miles added with a wink. 'Gives it away.'

'Besides, we still need to find Aggie and Miss Meriton,' piped up Clementine.

'And we're not going to let your father rot in jail,' Pearl muttered, pinning Diya's costume.

Cos took a shaky breath. 'I'msosorryforwhatIsaid,' she half cried, half shouted. 'It was mean, and cruel, but most of all it was untrue. You *are* my family. I don't know what I'd do without you all.'

Tears blurred Cos's vision, and before she knew it she was engulfed in a Dolly hug. A run-over toe and another pair of arms wrapped round her waist told her that Diya had joined in. Mary burst into tears, abandoning her filing to give Cos a squeeze. Miles put his handcuffs down and joined the group hug, followed by the other girls. Even Pearl reached out a finger to Cos's nose – like a Cat nose boop.

Finally they pulled apart, and Dolly caught sight of the calling card in Cos's hand. 'What's that?'

Cos had completely forgotten about her discovery. 'I know who the Spectre is,' she said. 'And you were right. It's not Mr Luminaire.'

'We know,' Mary said happily.

Cos frowned. 'You know?'

'When we got home, we asked the girls if they'd come across a child with the name Reynard when they were sorting out the old records,' Diya explained.

'And we had,' Dolly said cheerfully. 'A girl called Eunice. She entered the home aged ten, in 1886, but the matron sent her to a reformatory school just two years later.'

A memory tickled the edge of Cos's thoughts. 'I think I remember reading that record.'

'All Eunice's records were . . . sad,' Mary muttered. 'They said she was a troublemaker.'

'In fact, we even have a photo of her,' Ida signed, before linking arms with Cos and leading her over to the picture Miss Meriton had insisted be hung up. Ida pointed at a photo of a small, frowning girl on the far left of the group of identically dressed Home girls. She had wrapped her arms round herself, hugging herself tightly, and stood on her own.

As she stared at the photo of the dour-faced little girl, Cos felt a pang of empathy for Eunice. She knew all about being called a troublemaker – that had been Miss Stain's favourite nickname for her.

'Eunice had gout in her hands,' explained Mary. 'It's a kind of joint deformity, and it made using her hands painful.'

Cos let out a breath, holding out the Spectre's calling card so her friends could see. 'That's why her handwriting is so distinctive – her condition must make it hard to write.'

'And it's why Miss Fox is always wearing gloves,' added Pearl.

'That's not all we found out,' Miles said. 'Diya had another of her bright ideas.'

Diya grinned, her eyes flashing. 'Do you remember Aggie's fake names when we were planning the Treasure Palace Heist? Each one was different, but they all had the same meaning: unknown.'

Cos nodded, her thoughts racing to try to keep up with her clever friend's discovery.

'I asked Mary to look up what Reynard meant . . .'

'It's a medieval name for Fox,' Mary explained. She turned back to her desk and picked up another folder. Written in Mary's neat handwriting was *EVIDENCE THAT **MISS FOX** IS THE SPECTRE*. She handed the folder to Cos, who slipped the calling card into it.

'It's all going to add up. As soon as we find Aggie, I'll hand this over to her. But first we need to find the missing painting. It has to be somewhere inside the Spectacular.'

'But how do we get into the Spectacular?' Cos asked.

'We thought that was clear.' Pearl shrugged, gesturing to the costume rack. 'The Midnight Masquerade is a ball for the good and the great of London. We disguise ourselves as

guests! I've even forged us a fancy invitation . . .' She paused
her pinning and picked up a gold-edged piece of card, which
she showed Cos.

The plan Cos had been conjuring up on the walk home
from the jail slotted into place with the plotting her friends
had been doing in her absence.

'So we've got a way in, we know who the Spectre is, and
we've got a sort of plan.'

'We've also got these.' Diya held up an armful of what
looked like ordinary brown canisters. 'I think we've finally
cracked it! The very first silent fireworks.' She started
to hand one to each girl. 'We need to search the whole
Masquerade for the painting, so we'll need to split into
groups. If you find the stolen art, or get into trouble, just
pull hard on this.' Diya showed them the rope tail that hung
from each firework. 'That will launch a colourful explosion
into the sky, and will alert the rest of us so we can head in
your direction to help you. I've named them my Inaudible
Illuminations.'

'And don't forget about Miss Seymour's inspection,' piped
up Dolly. 'We have to ensure that we pass it *before* we leave
for the Masquerade. In fact, last night we decided to do
some crafting of our own that might help in that matter.' She
nodded at the other girls, and a gaggle of them disappeared
into the dining hall.

'To prove to Miss Seymour that the Star Diamond Home is incredible, she really needs to see the matron.'

Cos frowned. 'But that's impossible,' she spluttered. 'We don't know where Miss Meriton or Ag—'

The words died on Cos's lips as the girls returned. They were lugging a huge rope creation. As they neared Cos, she realised that the thing they were heaving looked approximately like a human: with gangly twisted limbs, a slumped head and coils of curly rope hair. For once in Cos's life, she was stunned into silence.

'It's nowhere nearly as good as your rope creations, Pearl,' Marnie added as she propped the rope head up, revealing painted eyes and lips. 'But we thought if we dress it in Miss Meriton's clothes and stick it in her office with the lights low we *might* be able to fool the inspector into thinking we have adult supervision.'

'That is . . .' Cos shook her head.

'INCREDIBLE,' Mary burst out.

'MAGNIFICENT,' Diya declared.

'TERRIFYING BUT WONDERFUL!' Miles shouted.

'Ingenious,' Pearl said quietly, stepping forward to give the fake matron a closer look. 'If we put some wiring in the neck, we can get her head to stand up on its own, and we might need to pad her out a little, but this is brilliant.'

The girls smiled at each other.

Pearl turned back to Cos. 'Now you've got to decide who you're going as.'

Cos grinned, her eyes flashing as she touched her father's locket. 'I already have someone in mind.'

CHAPTER TWENTY-FIVE

They worked feverishly all day. It was only when the shadows grew long and their stomachs started rumbling that Cos realised that evening, and Miss Seymour's inspection, would soon be upon them.

Pearl's hands hadn't stopped – she'd gone from measuring limbs to sewing gowns to painting faces to stitching pillows into the life-sized doll of Miss Meriton, which they'd now dressed in the matron's clothes. A team of girls toiled under her directions, and by the afternoon they'd finished their costumes. At the Midnight Masquerade they would be transformed into fearsome animals, characters from myth and legend, and heroes and heroines, past and present.

They'd heaved the fake Miss Meriton into her office, propping her on the sofa and covering her with blankets. One of the girls – Clare – was particularly skilled at voice imitation, and her impression of the absent matron was second to none. Cos hoped that with a very low-lit office, the real Miss Meriton's meticulous reports and Clare's uncanny ability to mimic, Miss Seymour wouldn't be able to tell the difference.

Mary spent the afternoon chalking her detailed map of the Spectacular on the blackboard. Miles used his thievery knowhow to scratch wobbly question marks on her map – highlighting the potential places where the Spectre might be hiding her stolen treasures. Diya had retreated to her invention station for the final tests on her Inaudible Illuminations. And Cos flitted from schoolroom to library to lab and back again, using her father's sewing tools to help where she could, her knee panging with pain.

Because she was concentrating so hard on making sure everything was prepared for the inspection, she almost failed to notice the shadow of a figure at the front door until it was too late. She shrieked in surprise. Her friends barrelled into the entrance foyer just as the handle creaked downwards and the door opened a crack.

Miles, Pearl and Mary darted towards the door, holding it shut, and Cos was able to catch a glimpse of the person trying to force their way into the Star Diamond Home.

Miss Seymour. From the Inspectorate of Children's Institutions.

'She's early,' Mary rasped as she strained to keep the inspector out. 'She's not due for another forty-five minutes!'

'We haven't fixed fake Miss Meriton's head yet!' a panicked Marnie squeaked.

'Or stashed our Masquerade costumes,' added Clare.

Cos glanced around at the finished costumes, draped over the banister of the rickety staircase, and the unused material and thread, still strewn across the floor.

'Aha, my instincts were right,' Miss Seymour said triumphantly. 'There is something mischievous happening in this institution!'

The inspector's foot stayed exactly where she'd placed it – wedged in between the door frame and the door. She leaned on the door in a gritted-teeth attempt to shove it open. Mary, Miles and Pearl tried desperately to hold her back.

'This is for your own good, children,' she insisted. 'I *must* inspect the Home and determine if you are being raised properly. I have a tight deadline to get my report back to the Inspectorate. This isn't creating a good first impression, you know!'

Cos *did* know. The word 'FAIL' was stuck in Cos's head, and she couldn't seem to shake it. That's what would happen when Miss Seymour eventually overpowered them and got inside – the Star Diamond Home would be no more. Tears welled in her eyes – her friends wouldn't be able to hold the inspector back for much longer. And, at that moment, a small girl with a steadfast gaze slipped under her arm.

'I have an idea. You lot go,' whispered Dolly, squeezing to the door. 'Grab your costumes. I'm going to open the door, and when she gets in you slip out. We'll do the inspection.' She had a mischievous glint in her eye – one that Cos recognised.

Cos could only nod. Miles, Mary and Pearl stepped back from the door and were replaced by a gaggle of the other girls. Cos and her friends rushed to pull their costumes over their uniforms.

'I won't give up, children,' Miss Seymour called from outside. 'I will get in this Home one way or another.'

'Three seconds, miss,' Dolly shouted. She looked at Cos and whispered, 'Are you ready?'

Cos nodded.

'One . . .' muttered Dolly.

Miss Seymour hammered on the door.

'Two . . .'

The inspector yanked the handle up and down.

'Three!'

The girls ran back from the door. It flew open, and Cos caught a glimpse of the surprised look on Miss Seymour's face as she tumbled inside.

Adrenaline shot through Cos as she slipped out of the front

door and down the ramp, followed by Diya, Miles, Mary and Pearl. They hurried down the street, heading in the direction of the Midnight Masquerade.

CHAPTER TWENTY-SIX

Cos straightened the collar of her costume, smoothing down the smart blouse and skirt. Its slit revealed a daring pair of baggy knickerbockers underneath. She adjusted her hat, touched her mother's handkerchief – which she had fashioned into a necktie – and gripped her walking stick, which had been secretly adapted for the purpose of their caper. Cos's outfit had been inspired by the photo of her mother Edmund kept in his locket.

Her friends had been similarly transformed. Diya's wheelchair was disguised as an automobile, and she was dressed as the first woman to drive a car, the inventor Bertha Benz. Pearl had decided to go as *The Lady Invalid*. She had carefully recreated the missing painting on her face, and fashioned a rectangular frame that surrounded her head.

Miles looked incredible as the escape artist and handcuff king Harry Houdini, and Mary had gone literal: she was dressed as an actual map – roads, hills and towns crisscrossed her body. Cos's chest puffed out with pride: not only were their costumes splendid, but she was sure that no one would figure out who they actually were.

As they approached the Spectacular, night had truly set in. The sky was inky black and dotted with stars. Cos's stomach lurched with nerves. Ahead of them, scores of horse-drawn carriages pulled up at the entrance, depositing fancily dressed ladies dripping in diamonds and gentlemen in jewel-encrusted cufflinks. The extravagant costumes made for perfect disguises – Cos spotted countless historical figures, kings and queens from days gone by, as well as famous artists, actors and writers.

She felt more nervous as they approached the entrance and waited not-so-patiently in line as the greasy-haired ticket attendant who had denied them entry only a few days before closely examined each invitation. Finally he nodded at the couple in front of them (dressed as Macbeth and Lady Macbeth) and turned his attention to Cos and her friends. Cos handed over the invitation Pearl had made, her hands trembling. The ticket attendant dragged his gaze over the children, and Cos prayed that he wouldn't recognise them. She held her breath as his eyes darted from the invitation to their costumes and back again. What if he saw Diya's spokes poking out? What if he recognised Cos's unruly tangle of hair? What if he judged Pearl's invitation a fake? Cos was ready to blurt out a furious riposte the moment the man denied them entry for a second time when, to her surprise, with a lazy nod, he gestured them in.

Cos's shock melted into indignant rage as her friends slipped into the Spectacular – when they were disguised as able-bodied, he was happy to let them in. But she had no time to dwell on that now. She had ladies to rescue and a painting to re-steal. Her mother's maxim repeated inside her head: *keep your feet on the ground, but always remember to look to the stars.*

Her friends gathered around her, and together they surveyed their surroundings. People thronged the Spectacular. A bandstand had been erected, and musicians strummed a gentle melody that spiralled through Earl's Court. Guests milled around, sipping champagne and picking hors d'oeuvres from the silver platters proffered by staff. Others screamed with delight as the fairground rides spun them round and round. It seemed to Cos as though the Midnight Masquerade was just like every other night at the Spectacular, except with rich people in fancy costumes. She couldn't quite see how it would benefit the London poor, but, if Miss Fox had anything to do with the event, it was probably a trick.

Cos didn't spot Miss Fox amongst the crowds, but she soon heard the booming guffaws of the Amazing Luminaire, who was dressed resplendently as the doomed King of France, Louis XVI. They spotted the unsmiling Madame Kaplinsky, clad in her usual spiritualist attire, and Gustav the Mighty, who made an impressive Hercules.

They ventured further into the Masquerade, the clink of glasses and fizz of champagne a constant backdrop. Cos led her friends to the shadows of a fairground wagon, near the carousel and away from the crowds, so they could talk without being overheard. As they put their heads together, a furry little creature appeared in the middle of their circle.

'Hello, Cat,' Pearl said. Mary leaned down to give the feline a stroke.

They allowed themselves to be distracted for a couple of minutes, until Cat spotted someone drop a lobster roll. She sprinted off, her bell dinging as she went. Cos watched her fluffy tail disappear into the sea of guests, then turned to her friends.

'Right, we need to split up and search. *The Lady Invalid* could be hidden anywhere in Earl's Court. There's far fewer of us than we'd planned, so we need to cover as much ground as quickly as possible. Miles and Mary – you take the Theatre of Illusions and the Great Wheel. Diya, Pearl and I will search the amusement rides.'

Diya handed Mary and Miles one Inaudible Illumination

each. 'When you find the painting, or if you get into trouble, set this off and we'll be right there,' she promised. 'And we'll do the same!'

Miles gave the trembling Mary a quick hug. 'Trouble? Pah! The greatest escapologist the world has ever known and a cartographer extraordinaire? This will be easy.'

Cos smiled at Mary. 'We can do this. We just need to keep our heads down and keep our cool. And try to avoid the Spectre,' she added a little hesitantly. Her words were as much for Mary as they were for herself.

With that, they split into two groups.

Cos soon realised that searching a fairground for a missing portrait was akin to searching for a needle in a haystack. The world blurred as she watched the carousel spin, and she closed her eyes, pushing away the smiling faces of the guests and the dizziness that threatened to engulf her. Time seemed to be getting away from them as they circled Earl's Court yet again, still with no idea where the painting had been concealed.

'This is pointless,' she said at last with a defeated shrug. 'We've searched all the rides in our search area at least twice. Short of rummaging through all the fairground wagons, we're no closer to finding the painting.'

'That's it!' Pearl exclaimed with such ferocity that Cos jumped. 'It's obvious.'

Diya and Cos blinked at her, confused.

Pearl sighed. 'Where in the Spectacular is all the important paperwork kept?'

'The theatre?' Diya suggested.

Pearl shook her head. 'The office wagon. The painting must be there!'

They rushed over to the fairground wagon that they'd hidden in on their first visit to the Spectacular. Cos's lock-picking skills weren't quite up to Miles's standard, but after a few attempts she managed to gain entry. The wagon was exactly the same as before: full of overstuffed bookshelves and reams of paperwork. With Diya waiting outside as a lookout, Cos and Pearl tore through the wagon in their search for *The Lady Invalid*.

'It's not here!' Cos cried, after searching for what felt like forever.

The wagon looked as though a tornado had hit it: folders were strewn across the narrow walkway, piles of books teetered on the desk and Cos had even upended the crate of old costumes. Stepping forward to right it, she slipped on a silk skirt, and, as she fell, her hand connected with something cold. She held on tightly, but whatever it was shifted under her grip. She closed her eyes and braced herself for impact, and landed flat on her back with a groan.

'What was that?' Diya called through the crack in the wagon door.

'I fell,' murmured Cos, making sure that all her joints were in their right place. To her relief, they were.

'That's not all you did,' Pearl exclaimed, carefully stepping over Cos. 'I think you might have found something.' She nodded towards the handle of the wood stove, which was pointing in a very odd direction.

That must've been what I grabbed hold of, Cos realised as she propped herself up on her elbows, frowning at Pearl's discovery. *It looks like a . . . lever.*

Pearl stooped and yanked the handle back. Inside the stove, there was a loud *clunk*. 'There's something in there,' she said, her eyes glinting.

Pearl held out her hand to help Cos up. Her heart thumping, Cos opened the stove door. Inside were the sooty remains of a fire. Pearl pulled the lever again, and a strange contraption thudded downwards from its hiding place in the stove's chimney. A small strongbox was nestled inside the contraption.

Cos's mouth fell open.

'What did you find?' Diya asked.

'The Spectre has built a kind of lift to hide a small safe,' Pearl explained, 'inside the stove.'

'And does the safe have the painting in it?' Diya demanded.

Pearl shrugged. Cos sucked in a nervous breath and reached for the strongbox, pulling it from its grimy home.

Cradling it, she readied herself to pick its lock, but to her surprise it clicked open easily. Jumbled inside were piles of stolen trinkets, just like they'd found in the mansion, and nestled between brackets and brooches was a rolled-up canvas: *The Lady Invalid*.

Cos let out a hiss of triumph.

'We've found it!' Pearl exclaimed. Cos quickly unscrewed the handle of her brand-new walking stick, crafted for her by Pearl. Inside, the walking stick was completely hollow – the perfect place to store their re-stolen painting. Pearl picked up the artwork carefully and slotted it neatly into Cos's stick.

Cos ran a hand over the jumble of items, and her fingers touched something that looked familiar. *Diya's missing spanner.* She rummaged through the pile a little longer, desperately searching for her star clip, but it wasn't there, although she did uncover Mary's silver pocket watch. She kept both items, intending to reunite them with their rightful owners soon.

Rat-a-tat-tat. Diya knocked smartly on the wagon door. 'Er, I think we need to hurry up. I've spotted Miss Fox.'

Cos and Pearl clattered out of the fairground wagon, moving as fast as their legs would carry them. Miss Fox wore an emerald-green gown. She was stalking the Spectacular as if she were searching for someone.

'The theatre,' Diya suggested, as Cos tucked her friend's hammer back into her tool bag. 'We can hide there, send up an Inaudible Illumination, meet the others and get out of here.'

Breathlessly, Cos nodded, and they rushed in the direction of the fluttering theatre tent. But, as they weaved through the throng, Pearl was swept up in the crowd jostling for the next carousel ride. She whimpered and tried to reach out for Cos, but they were too far away. Cos and Diya watched helplessly as their friend was barged on to the carousel platform. An ear-splitting, jaunty tune was playing; Pearl wrapped her arms round herself, her eyes shut, shivering.

'I'm coming, Pearly,' Cos promised, summoning up the courage to take the big step on to the carousel. She threaded her way past the chariots and horses as Diya watched nervously from the ground. She stepped close to the shaking Pearl, grabbed the ear defenders from her satchel and slid them over her ears.

'It's all right, Pearl,' Cos whispered, hoping her friend could hear her over the carousel noise.

She clamped one hand tightly round a pole and her other round Pearl's shoulders as the ride began to turn. The world blurred as they spun, and Cos closed her eyes. It felt as if the ride went on forever, but finally it began to slow. Cos opened her eyes and scanned her surroundings. The other guests hopped from their steeds and slipped from the carousel. Cos allowed herself a deep, gulping breath. Now they just needed to get to the theatre.

A little off-kilter, Cos and Pearl stumbled towards Diya. They were so close! But then Cos spotted Miss Fox storm out of her wagon, her eyes wild. She stared right at Cos, and began to march towards her.

CHAPTER TWENTY-SEVEN

'**Y**OU!' hissed Miss Fox, pointing a trembling finger in Cos's direction. 'I knew something was off about your costumes. They're far too clever to be thought up by this gaggle of aristocrats.' She weaved past the frozen gryphons and unicorns that populated the carousel. 'I've seen three Queen Elizabeths in the last ten minutes. People have absolutely no imagination.'

Cos and Pearl backed up, Cos holding her walking stick – and its hidden treasures – tightly.

Miss Fox cleared her throat. 'This is a private ride,' she announced to the Masquerade attendees who were milling around the carousel. 'The carousel will reopen to guests in a moment.'

All the other riders left the carousel, leaving Cos and Pearl to the Spectre's mercy. Diya let out a strangled cry.

'I know you've stolen my painting,' Miss Fox muttered as she turned back to Cos, grudging admiration on her face. 'But I need it back. It's my reward, you see, for the years I spent in that draughty, loveless Home.' Miss Fox smiled sweetly, as if she'd just offered them a cup of tea. She came to a stop a few steps from Cos and Pearl. A shiver crept up Cos's spine, but she held Pearl's hand tightly. The girls glowered at the criminal.

Miss Fox glanced behind her, towards the Theatre of Illusions. Cos thought she caught a flicker of something in the con woman's eyes – doubt, maybe, or fear?

'I don't have much time.' Miss Fox snapped her fingers impatiently. 'Hand me the painting – *now*.'

Silence answered her. In fact, Cos, Pearl and Diya had said nothing since the fraudster had spotted them.

Miss Fox sighed dramatically, as though she were a nursemaid trying to cajole toddlers into eating vegetables. 'I didn't want to have to do this.' One of her hands moved like a flash towards a lever attached to the central console of the carousel. She shifted it down, and with an almighty creak the carousel slowly began to turn, nearly knocking Cos off balance, and sending Pearl jolting into a nearby horse. Pearl groaned as the carousel lit up with her on it for the second time.

'This is the first speed,' said Miss Fox through gritted teeth. 'But unless I get my possessions back I won't hesitate to go faster. You are already unsteady. I wonder what would happen if your poor legs slipped and your little bodies were crushed under the mechanism.'

That thought turned Cos's legs to jelly. She gripped her walking stick even more tightly as she grappled for the right words.

'They aren't your possessions, though.' Pearl's words rang out, honest and loud, and she fixed the thief with a hard stare. Pride rose up in Cos's chest. Pearl was battling so much – loud noises, flashing lights and the floor spinning beneath her feet, yet she was still determined to stand up for what was right.

Miss Fox blinked, as if surprised. Before she answered, she pushed the lever up another gear. The world began to spin a little faster, and the Spectacular blurred in front of Cos's eyes.

'Surely *you* can understand. Every time anyone saw my hands, they'd flinch. I was deemed "hopelessly crippled". They told me I would spend my entire life in an institution. It was one crushing blow after another. I was constantly reminded that I would only ever be an *unfortunate* . . .' Her voice cracked, and she wrung her gloved hands.

Cos felt a pang of sympathy. Miss Fox had been abandoned by the people who were supposed to care for her most, had been told she was unworthy of love. Cos suddenly had the overwhelming urge to hug her.

But Miss Fox saw her pitying gaze, and her face twisted into a scowl. She clicked the lever up one more notch. The carousel was more than spinning now – it was so fast Cos could feel her knees wobbling dangerously in her kneecaps. The friends held each other more tightly, and Miss Fox had to shout over the noise of the carousel to be heard.

'I made a promise to myself that I would defy all their expectations of me. I would build a better life. A life full of beauty – full of all the things I never had. My childhood may have been stolen, but being the Spectre allowed me to reclaim what I was owed. I proved everyone wrong. I fulfilled every wish the younger me had dreamed up. All except one: owning a priceless piece of art. *The Lady Invalid* seemed fated to be mine. She was an innovative visionary who bent the world to her will, refusing to be held back by her unfortunateness. How magical that you can glean all of that from the painting!'

'But if you love being the Spectre so much, then why did you frame my father?' asked Cos.

'I didn't intend to, originally. I planned to keep going – travelling the world and stealing treasures. But that pesky journalist got too close to the truth, and then I carelessly mislaid the map for the Siraj elephant. I had to act swiftly. It was nothing personal, but Mr Deans was the perfect scapegoat.'

Cos's thoughts whirled. *Journalist? That had to be Aggie.* Before she could question the Spectre further, Miss Fox carried on.

'That's when I decided to change course. Give everything up, so to speak. Burn it to the ground and start again.'

'I don't understand.' Cos's words were whipped away in the wind, just as a horrifying smell reached her nostrils. 'Do you mean *actually* burn?'

Miss Fox nodded, a grimace playing over her lips. 'Tonight there will be a tragic accidental fire. The Spectacular will burn, and poor mousy Miss Fox will perish, alongside a rather unfortunate journalist who didn't keep her nose out of my business, and her lady friend. The Spectacular's demise and Mr Dean's arrest will tie up all my loose ends.'

Cos gasped. Aggie and Miss Meriton were here somewhere – taken captive by the Spectre – and the Spectre planned to kill them!

'And tomorrow I will begin anew,' Miss Fox continued. 'The insurance money will be more than enough for me to finish building my mansion and start a brand-new life. After the museum, I realised it's too risky to keep being the Spectre, especially now that someone else has taken the fall for my crimes.'

As Miss Fox's words sank in, Cos's heart began to thump. Her gaze drifted upwards as she and her friends spun round and round, and she caught a glimpse of flames licking up the side of the Theatre of Illusions. She stared in horror, her feet frozen to the creaking boards of the carousel. The fire spread impossibly fast, crackling down the tent hungrily. In no time at all, it would reach all the rides and attractions that dotted Earl's Court. Cos glanced around. The Masquerade guests were oblivious, chatting and laughing as the acrid smoke curled upwards. It would only be a matter of time before they realised the danger they were in. Cos couldn't pull her gaze away. Miss Fox had done this on purpose – torched her own event.

Cos thought of Mary, Miles, Miss Meriton and Aggie. What would happen when the flames reached them, wherever they were? Would they be able to escape? Or would the fire consume them too? Cos's hands balled into fists as the fire burned through the velvet of the tent.

'She started as Eunice Reynard, then became Miss Fox,' Pearl continued, pausing to suck in a Mary-like breath. Cos noticed that smoke was already swirling in the air around them. 'She's probably got a whole new identity already lined up . . .'

'You really are clever, aren't you?' Miss Fox rasped. 'But it doesn't matter. The fire is already ripping through Earl's Court, destroying all evidence of my past and my crimes. The only thing I want to keep is in your possession. So.' She paused dramatically, gripping the carousel lever. 'I will ask you all one more time and one more time only. Give me my painting.'

'There are hundreds of people here!' Cos cried. 'You're putting everyone's lives in danger – including yours. Is it really worth it?'

For a split second, doubt flashed across the con woman's face. Then she snarled, 'Give me the painting.'

In quick succession, three things happened.

Miss Fox lunged towards Pearl. As she did, Cat leaped into her path, knocking her off balance. A strangled cry escaped from Miss Fox's throat as she fell.

Pearl yanked the carousel lever back, jolting the ride to a sudden, bone-shaking halt. Cos and Pearl were tossed around like waves in a storm. The fall rattled Cos's joints something dreadful. Her head collided with the floor, and she saw stars.

Then a light exploded in the sky. A firework had been set off.

Diya's face paled as she locked eyes with Cos. 'They're in trouble,' she said, her voice high-pitched and panicked.

'It's probably because of the fire,' Cos said, hoping beyond hope that she was right.

'Look!' Pearl was standing, pointing at the Great Wheel, silhouetted against the star-strewn sky. There, in the distance, Cos could just about make out two figures dangling from the carriage that hung at the highest point of the wheel. An unearthly scream erupted from her.

Mary and Miles.

CHAPTER TWENTY-EIGHT

Cos's world shifted into slow motion. She painfully pulled herself to her feet, her teeth gritted. Pearl and Diya were already careening away from the carousel, Diya's wheels moving so fast that her costume rode up and her spokes blurred. Cos tried to follow as fast as she could, but she was going against the grain. Hundreds of elaborately costumed guests fled towards her, fear across their faces, in a desperate attempt to escape the rapidly approaching flames. Cos stumbled onwards, past kings, explorers and heroes, keeping Pearl and Diya in her line of sight.

By the time Cos reached the base of the Great Wheel, the air was hot and choking, and the ride operators had – understandably – abandoned their stations. The wheel was still turning, but its steel structure was worryingly close to the rapidly approaching flames. Dangling from the topmost carriage by his fingertips was Miles, and hanging on to his ankle was a screeching Mary. Cos gasped. If Miles let go now, they would surely fall to their death.

As one of the carriages docked at the platform, Cos realised that there were still people trapped inside, banging on the glass walls. As Cos wiped the sweat from her forehead, Diya deployed her Rambunctious Ramp, wheeled up to the platform and used her spanner to lever open the door, freeing the people from the passenger car. They rushed past the girls, heading towards the exit.

Cos fought against the fleeing rabble, staggering up the ramp. Diya had already started rifling through the bag attached to the back of her wheelchair, lobbing out various contraptions. Finally she came across the device she wanted: the Great Grabber. Her jaw clenched, Diya sped back down the ramp, turned back to face the wheel and put on her brake.

She closed one eye and held the metal tube up to her cheek, aiming it skywards. As Diya concentrated, Pearl plucked her abandoned spanner from the platform floor, just as the empty carriage soared away, to be replaced by another filled with terrified passengers. Pearl cranked the spanner, opening the carriage door. Another group of people flooded out.

Diya fired her Great Grabber. The rope soared through the

air towards the wheel, and its hook caught round the spoke nearest to Miles and Mary. Diya held tightly to the other end of the Grabber. She pulled her end of the rope taut, creating a zip line that extended from the spoke near to their friends to the ground. Diya tied her end of the rope round a nearby lamp post.

Then Miles began to shunt himself and Mary sideways, closer to the zip line. They would be able to slide down the rope to safety.

'Cos, can we switch?' Pearl asked, holding out Diya's spanner. 'I have an idea.'

Cos nodded, taking the tool. She leaned her walking stick against the platform and limped forward, opening the door of the latest docked carriage. People rushed past her, eager to escape the fire.

Pearl pulled her knitted blanket from her satchel. She and Diya each took two corners, holding it taut. They had created a soft landing for Miles and Mary.

Cos peered up, just as Miles swung one arm from the wheel spoke to the zip line. He tipped his hat, looping it round the cable, before grabbing the other side, creating a handhold he could use to slide towards the ground.

Mary gave a deafening screech as she held on to Miles and they careened down the zip line together. They thudded into Pearl's blanket and tumbled to the ground. Relief flooded through Cos but, to her shock, her friends' faces were full of worry.

'Miss Meriton and Aggie,' rasped Miles. 'We found them, and I managed to slip my lockpick under the door. But, before we could help more, a gust of wind knocked us off balance.'

Mary raised a shaking hand to point at the broken carriage with the blacked-out windows. The broken carriage – the one they hadn't been allowed on, on the first day they visited the Spectacular. It was the perfect place to hide a troublesome journalist and matron.

As the final carriage full of people docked at the platform and Cos released them, Miss Fox raced towards the wheel, grabbing a lever and pulling it. All of a sudden, the wheel stopped moving, trapping Aggie and Miss Meriton's carriage high above the ground.

Cos's feet moved before her brain had fully thought things through. She glared up at the star-strewn sky, the only light the fire. Cos sucked in a deep breath and reached up, trying to grip the slick surface of the wheel. But her fingers slipped off before she could heft herself higher. Behind her, the Theatre of Illusions collapsed into itself.

Prove her father's innocence; catch the Spectre; rescue Aggie and Miss Meriton. Those things seemed utterly impossible now. If the fire at Earl's Court continued, the Spectre would have burned away all evidence of her guilt, and

Cos, her friends and their favourite adults would be consumed by the flames.

Cos reached up again. This time, she did it. She heaved herself higher, her feet scrambling to find purchase. She gritted her teeth and pulled herself higher still, and finally found a toehold. Her back screamed with pain, but Cos set her jaw and again reached upwards. Slowly but surely, she was closing in on the broken carriage.

The fire burned bright on the horizon, but still Cos climbed.

And then she slipped.

For a moment, Cos held on by her fingertips, her legs kicking uselessly in the wind. She glanced downwards, towards the toy town of London. Her nails were tearing as she fought to hold on, but she knew it was a losing battle – she was going to fall. And she was only a handhold or two from reaching the carriage.

Just as she was about to surrender to the inevitable, two figures suddenly appeared above her and held out their hands. Cos gasped as Miss Meriton and Aggie pulled her to safety.

There was no time for an emotional reunion. Cos pointed towards Diya's zip line, and the two women nodded. They tiptoed unsteadily along the wooden arm of the Wheel, from the carriage towards the rope. Cos's stomach lurched with every step – the ground seemed awfully far away. When they reached the rope, Cos insisted that the adults go first, and for once they didn't argue. As soon as Aggie and Miss Meriton were safely on the ground, Cos breathed a sigh of relief. Just as she was about to follow them, someone yanked hard on Cos's hair. Cos turned to see the Spectre glaring back at her. She must have scaled the wheel, just like Cos, in an effort to retrieve her stolen treasures. Cos struggled to escape, but Miss Fox wrapped her arms round her chest, crushing the breath out of her. The carriage nearest to the theatre was engulfed in flames now, and the fire was beginning a rapid ascent up the wheel's wooden structure. Cos baulked. Soon the entire wheel would be alight.

'Give me my painting,' Miss Fox hissed.

Cos's gaze flicked, unbidden, to the ground, to her trusty walking stick, which she had abandoned on the platform below. 'I don't have it,' Cos wheezed, managing to land a blow in between Miss Fox's ribs.

There was an almighty crash as the burning carriage

fell to the ground.

The con artist grunted, and Cos used that moment to twist herself free. She hurried to the centre shaft of the wheel, risking a glance behind her. Miss Fox, teeth bared, was following her. Cos knew she didn't have much time. The fire was tracing a crescent moon of flame up the wheel: its wooden planks burned brightly before splintering into charcoaled skeletons. The heat was blistering.

The rope cable that Diya had fired towards the wheel was still taut, stretching down towards the ground. But the fire was snaking ever closer. As soon as the rope was aflame, Cos would have no chance of getting safely to the ground.

She dug her hands in the pocket that she insisted Pearl insert in all of their costumes, and withdrew one of her most treasured possessions: the handkerchief that had once belonged to her mother. The one her father had carefully stitched back together. She hoped this wouldn't destroy his work.

'Everyone's been evacuated from the wheel!' Diya's shout was almost whipped away by the wind.

Cos pulled the handkerchief taut, twisting the material into a rope.

Her friends were gathered below, all safe, their faces twisted with fear. Miss Meriton and Aggie had collapsed in a heap on the ground, exhausted from their imprisonment.

Cos looped her newly constructed rope over Diya's zip line.

Miles shook his head, nudging the others and pointing towards Cos.

'COS!' Mary screeched. 'PLEASE HURRY!'

Cos held on tightly to her handkerchief, her mother's saying running through her head: *keep your feet on the ground, but always remember to look to the stars*. Cos had never wanted to be on solid ground more.

Pearl's hands flapped with nerves. Miss Meriton and Aggie held each other.

Cos looked to the stars. And then she jumped.

She arced through the air, the wind whooshing past her. The world around her blurred into nothing as she clung desperately to her makeshift pulley. Then, with a sickeningly sudden thud, Cos hit Pearl's blanket, which cushioned her landing slightly, and let go of her handkerchief, crashing to the ground in a tangle of limbs.

CHAPTER TWENTY-NINE

Stars twinkled in Cos's eyes, the only light she could see amongst the yawning black. Pain ricocheted through her, and she was only partly aware that her limbs were twitching uncontrollably. A guttural scream erupted from her throat, but only she could hear it – the roar of the fleeing Spectacular patrons covered up her shouts. Even as she lay there, frightened people pushed past her in their hurry to escape the fire.

Acrid smoke drifted up Cos's nostrils. *This is it,* she thought. *I'm trapped.* She would never get to see Pearl smile again, or test out one of Miles's new magic tricks, or – and this hurt most of all – tell her father she loved him.

Cos blinked out a tear, and the blurry world began to come back into focus. As people fled, several familiar figures elbowed their way towards her. They gathered around her, forming a protective barrier. Mary, Diya, Miles, Pearl, Miss Meriton and Aggie.

Miss Meriton's face paled as she looked at Cos's knee, twisted at a very unnatural angle. She swallowed and grabbed Cos's hand. 'Cos. Listen to me. You need to *relax*.'

Every muscle in Cos's body was as taut as a violin string. Sweat beaded on her forehead, and tears streamed down her cheeks. She glanced down at her kneecap, which bulged on the wrong side of her leg. She felt her eyes roll back in her head. But she wouldn't – she couldn't – let unconsciousness take her. Cos gritted her teeth, sucking in a deep breath.

Miss Meriton squeezed Cos's hand, and Cos's gaze flickered from her horrible, misshapen leg towards the matron's crystal-blue eyes.

'That's it,' Miss Meriton encouraged, her voice calm and slow. 'In and out.'

Cos did as Miss Meriton said, focusing on her breathing. After a few moments, she was able to glance at her leg and not feel as if she might lose the contents of her stomach. Determination took hold. Scowling, Cos pushed herself up on her elbows. With a grunt, she lifted her arm and brought her elbow down hard on her kneecap, knocking it back into place. As the pain ebbed away, Cos grabbed her knees and hugged them against her chest.

Miss Meriton and Aggie buried their heads in Cos's

unruly tangle of hair, holding her tight.

'You did it,' breathed Miss Meriton.

'I couldn't have, without you all,' Cos muttered, wiping her tears on her sleeve as she gingerly bent and straightened her leg. It throbbed in pain, but it was nowhere near as bad as when the joint was out. 'It's horrible when it gets stuck like that . . .'

As Cos spoke, she realised that the crowd had thinned considerably, leaving only a few stragglers making for the Spectacular's many exits. She spotted some familiar people – the strongman, the ghost whisperer, the patron – running from the flames. Most of them coughed into their scarves; the fog of grey smoke hung heavy in the air. It stung her eyes and throat. The fire had spread remarkably fast, blazing along the temporary walls that marked the boundary of Earl's Court, destroying the far-off rides and carousels of the fairground. The Great Wheel – which Cos had been dangling from only minutes before – was now completely alight, like a gigantic Catherine wheel. The air was stuffy and stiflingly hot.

Aggie and Miss Meriton took one of Cos's arms each and hoisted her to standing. Mary handed her back her trusty walking stick. Cos didn't risk putting any weight on her injured leg. Slowly, with her friends by her side, Cos limped in the same direction as the other stragglers, towards the exit. She had a firm grasp of her walking stick – which had hidden within it the stolen-back artwork taken by the Spectre. They stumbled onwards in silence for a few minutes as the Spectacular burned down around them.

'Aggie,' croaked Cos as the shadowy turnstiles came into view. 'Tell us how you figured out that Miss Fox was the Spectre. It'll help distract me from the pain.'

Aggie nodded, blowing a stray tendril of hair from her forehead as she supported Cos. 'You girls and Miles know that I can never resist a good mystery so when a very old friend, Teddy, wrote to me and told me he'd received the most dastardly anonymous threat, I knew I had to investigate. It soon became clear to me that the threat Teddy had received was bound up with a travelling funfair called the Spectacular. I quickly noticed another strange coincidence: that the Spectre struck in every city that the Spectacular visited.'

'We came to the same conclusion!' Mary muttered breathlessly.

'As soon as I arrived back in London, I began looking into the Spectacular,' Aggie continued. 'But I struggled to find anything incriminating, so I decided to fall back on an old investigative technique: going undercover.'

'How did the police never find the connection between the thief and the Spectacular?' Miles asked.

Aggie crooked an eyebrow. 'Because the Spectacular is the perfect cover for criminality.'

'What does that mean?' said Cos.

'Criminals often have fronts,' answered Miles, his face twisted as though he were recalling a sad memory. 'They buy a legitimate business and use it as a base for wrongdoing. Police aren't going to think about looking for stolen jewels in a butcher's shop.'

'*Exactly*,' hissed Aggie as she adjusted Cos's weight on her shoulder. 'And if you're an international thief, wouldn't a travelling funfair be the perfect cover?'

There was a murmur of realisation.

Cos thought for a beat, pain throbbing with every step. 'So is your friend Teddy Sir Theodore Vincent?'

'Yes,' Aggie replied. 'Ted and I go back aeons.'

'And does he have something to do with the horrible note we found on your desk?'

Aggie stopped walking, her eyebrows raised and a wry smile on her face. 'You found that? I shouldn't be surprised, really – you lot are the cleverest children I know. Yes, Teddy received that note. He was being blackmailed, and I was the only person he could trust to investigate it discreetly.'

'Why?' Pearl whispered.

Aggie thrust her free hand into her dress. 'I hid half of the note in my desk, just in case my undercover investigation went awry. But I kept the other half with me, because the information within it was of a sensitive nature.' She pulled out

a crumpled piece of paper, ripped at the top, and held it out
so they all could see.

1. SUPPORT THE SPECTACULAR.
2. EXHIBIT *THE LADY INVALID.*
COMPLY FOR THE SAKE OF YOUR FORBIDDEN
LOVE.

The Spectre had signed the note with a flourish. Put
together with the half of the note they'd found, it read:

AGREE TO MY DEMANDS OR I WILL EXPOSE YOUR
SECRET FOR ALL THE WORLD TO SEE.
1. OFFER THE SPECTACULAR YOUR PATRONAGE.
2. EXHIBIT *THE LADY INVALID.*
COMPLY FOR THE SAKE OF YOUR FORBIDDEN
LOVE.

'Well, that explains one mystery,' Mary muttered. 'How
the painting ended up in a funfair, of all places.'

'But what is this "forbidden love"?' Diya asked. 'And
why were *you* the only person he could trust to investigate
it?'

'Because, like Teddy, I have also experienced forbidden
love.' In the glow of the flames, Cos saw the tips of Aggie's ears
turn red. 'Love that is – wrongly, in my opinion – sometimes
seen as a sin: women who love women, and men who love
men.'

Aggie locked eyes with Miss Meriton, and a realisation

hit Cos like a lightning bolt. The two women spent most evenings and weekends together. Miss Meriton was the only person Aggie trusted with knowledge of her investigations. They even wore matching silver rings on the fourth finger of their left hands. How had she missed it?

'You're in love with each other?' she gasped.

The women thought for a beat, then nodded.

'Some men seem to think that the fairer sex are completely unaware of such a love, and that if it is never spoken about then we'll never find out. It's nonsense, of course,' said Miss Meriton softly.

Aggie smiled, her eyes watery. 'Love always finds a way.'

For once, Cos and her friends were stunned into silence. There was only a gentle *swish-swish* as Pearl's paintbrush swept across her forearm.

'What are you painting, Pearly?' Aggie asked.

Pearl held up her arm. There was now a miniature portrait of Aggie and Miss Meriton in the crook of her elbow, gazing lovingly at each other. 'It's just a sketch at the moment, but I promise I'll make you both a locket so that you can always have each other close.'

Miss Meriton's voice came out all wobbly. 'That's beautiful, Pearl. Thank you.'

'If two people love each other, then that ought to be the end of the matter,' Diya concluded decisively. Cos knew she was thinking of her parents, who had been unable to marry, simply because her father didn't follow the 'right' religion.

'Agreed,' Mary said firmly.

'Thirded,' Miles added.

'Love should be celebrated,' croaked Cos – half because of the smoke caught in her throat, and half because of the strange mixture of joy, sadness and fear she felt for the matron and the journalist – 'in all its forms. Just promise me you won't start leaving love poems around the Home – I had enough of that with my parents.'

Aggie unsuccessfully stifled a cackle and squeezed Cos's shoulder. 'We promise!'

'So who is Teddy in love with?' Mary asked.

'He lives very happily with a lovely gentleman,' Miss Meriton explained. 'They have been together for a number of years and have had no trouble – that was, until the note.'

'Exactly,' said Aggie. 'After I discovered the connection between the Spectacular and the Spectre, I concluded that the person who sent the note *had* to be the Spectre, and that meant that he was after *The Lady Invalid*. It fitted perfectly with the Spectre's other known crimes – he was targeting one-of-a-kind priceless items. So Teddy and I decided we would stop the Spectre once and for all. I went undercover at the Spectacular as a ride attendant on the Great Wheel, and waited to see if we could stake out the Spectre. I started investigating my colleagues and, although many of them had secrets, I couldn't pinpoint who the criminal mastermind was. It wasn't until I followed Miss Fox one night that I realised it was her.'

'How did you figure it out?' Diya asked.

'I spied her opening a cleverly concealed strongbox in the office wagon. I wasn't unduly suspicious – it was perfectly legitimate for the Spectacular to have a strongbox on site. But, just in case, I waited for her to leave and, utilising the lock-picking skills Miles had taught me, I sneaked inside to examine the strongbox. I couldn't work out exactly how to open it, but Miss Fox had been somewhat careless when she was depositing her ill-gotten gains that night. She had dropped a one-of-a-kind item I immediately recognised on the floor of the wagon: a star clip.'

Aggie held up Cos's mother's precious keepsake, and handed it to Cos. Cos gasped, and slipped it into her hair.

'But that wasn't my biggest discovery . . .' Aggie withdrew a small notebook hidden within her blouse and handed it to Mary. 'After I found the star, I decided to have a closer look at the paperwork on Miss Fox's desk. Like me, she's fond of hiding important things in false-bottomed stationery organisers.'

'This looks just like the exercise books we use in school.'

Mary brushed its leather-cracked cover and opened it.

They all strained to see what Aggie had found. Written in the Spectre's now-familiar spiky handwriting were the words:

The journal of Eunice Reynard, age 12.

Resident at the Home for Unfortunate Girls, Kensington

Mary flicked to the next page of scribbled notes, which was headed *Things I wish I could have*. As Cos scanned the list, a painful lump formed in her throat. The first couple of wishes were jotted down in pencil, with misspelled words and crossings-out – they had obviously been written by someone just learning how to write.

1. A bed that ~~is'nt~~ isn't hard as nails.
2. A ~~comfeet comfitit~~ not-itchy blanket that actually keeps me warm.
3. Stockings without holes.
4. Never having to eat ~~grewl~~ gruel again

Cos's heart squeezed tightly. She had wished for all those things time and time again in the years she'd spent growing up with the Stains. Despite everything, she felt awful for Eunice.

The next few points were written in a splotchy midnight-black ink that had splattered over the page. The handwriting was still just as scribbly, but Cos knew from experience that schoolchildren were only allowed to use pens and ink when they were older. Eunice's wish list seemed to have been written over years.

67. Parents that visit
68. A silk pair of gloves (to hide my unfortunate-ness)
69. A beautiful doll of my very own (shop-bought)

Again Cos understood. On the rare occasions that she didn't need her mobility aids, Cos revelled in being invisible. When she used her stick, or her Wonderful Wheelchair, the constant stares and whispers from complete strangers were tiresome.

And she also knew the pain of being the only girl in the Home who didn't have a visitor. She sighed. Maybe if Eunice had been at the Home fourteen years later, she and Cos could have been friends.

The list continued, this time written in blue ink.

✓ 101. A ball gown
✓ 102. A diamond necklace
   103. A butler
   104. A magnificent estate

Cos noticed that some of the wishes had ticks next to them — as though they had been achieved. Mary flicked the page over, revealing hundreds more wishes. Cos's gaze flitted from wish to wish. Eunice's dreams had changed every time she added to her list: from hoping away the spartan and cold upbringing she had in the Home, to longing for possessions that belonged solely to her, to coveting the kind of life that only princesses and heiresses had.

'She's ticked off what she'd already stolen,' said Pearl, pointing to a line that read **168. A priceless piece of art**.

Cos thought back to how much she'd once admired the Spectre and their audacious spree of thievery, thinking that another heist might secure the Home's future. But now she could see how easily that desire for a better life could be twisted into callous greed and stealing for stealing's sake. Cos never wanted to become *that* kind of criminal. She wanted to be the good kind: a thief that pilfered the already-stolen, an outlaw who righted the wrongs the rich usually got away with, a troublemaker – in the best kind of way.

'This list is almost never-ending!' Mary was aghast.

Aggie nodded. 'Exactly – and it's proof that Miss Fox, alias Eunice Reynard, is the Spectre. Unfortunately, I was so consumed with my discovery that I'd neglected to be aware of my surroundings.' Aggie sucked in a deep breath. 'Before I could do so, I was struck with something hard, and lost consciousness. When I came to, I was chained up, blindfolded and gagged. I knew I was somewhere in the Spectacular, because I could hear the crowds. I also suspected I was on one of the rides, because my prison cell moved. A day after I was imprisoned, someone else was shoved into my cell – Cora. She was the only person I had trusted with my location. When she woke, she told me that Miss Fox had attacked her when she questioned her about my whereabouts. She told me that the Van Hackenboeck had been stolen, and that Edmund had been arrested for its theft. We were both injured and scared, but we knew the truth: Edmund was innocent.'

A sad silence settled over the group as everyone digested Aggie's words. The silence was broken only by a distant crash as the Great Wheel succumbed to the flames and collapsed in a twist of wood. Cos felt her knee wobble dangerously, and she bent down to hold her joint in place before they began their slow walk again. Everything weighed upon Cos all at once: the fire, the revelations about the Spectre and most of all her father's wrongful imprisonment.

'Unfortunately, we had no way to escape.' Miss Meriton took over the explanation. 'We were barely fed – often we'd wake up to mouldy bread being shoved in the carriage.' She shivered. 'Luckily for us, we had you all. We never lost faith that you would rescue us.'

As they approached the turnstiles, Cos allowed herself a sigh of relief. They'd done it – rescued Aggie and Miss Meriton *and* reverse-heisted the Spectre.

Just a few more steps, she thought.

Cos saw a shadow of something out of the corner of her eye: the next moment, two figures hurtled towards her.

Miss Fox was a twisted ghost of her former self: her dress ripped and scorched, her eyes wide and her cheeks sunken like a skeleton. Sobs ripped from Gideon Luminaire's throat as he turned to stare at his burning Spectacular. He was still dressed in his King Louis XVI costume – a white ermine fur collar laid over a silk shirt, bouffant breeches and buckled shoes – but ash dusted his ermine and his shirt was untucked.

'Miss Fox, Miss Fox, I beseech you to help me!' He went to take his assistant's hand, but she shoved him away. 'My Spectacular burns.'

'I think you'll find that it's *my* Spectacular,' growled Miss Fox. She turned towards Cos, her eyes blazing with rage. 'Where is the painting?'

Cos gripped her walking stick as Miss Meriton and Aggie stepped in front of her, shielding Cos and her friends.

The Amazing Luminaire went slack as a realisation hit him. 'Oh my goodness. I signed over controlling shares in the Spectacular to you because the debtors' prison was after me. But it was all a lie.' He sobbed, then turned to face his secretary. 'It's *you*. You're the Spectre.'

'Of course I am, you dunce.' Miss Fox reached into her handbag, and withdrew a pearl-encrusted pistol, which she pointed in Cos's direction. The breath left Cos's body as she stared down the barrel of the gun.

'Hand it over now, or I'll start shooting you all. One by one.'

Time seemed to slow as Cos, leaning heavily on Pearl and Mary for support, began to unscrew the handle of her hollow walking stick. She could hear the spit and crackle of the fire in her ears, feel the Midnight Masquerade guests rush past her towards the exit and see the light glinting off the pearly gun. Shaking, she reached down into the hiding place, fingers brushing the paper-thin canvas. Ever so carefully, she pulled out the stolen treasure and held it out to the Spectre.

A desperate sort of triumph flashed across Miss Fox's gaunt face. But before she could grab the painting a shadow leaped through the air, knocking the pistol from the Spectre's grip and sending it clattering to the ground.

It was Cat! The feline's gaze was trained on the light reflected from the pearl-encrusted weapon, her paws batting at it on the ground. Miss Fox snarled. But before she could recover her gun or snatch the stolen items Cos spotted several horse-drawn fire engines approaching the turnstiles, each staffed with a dozen firefighters. As the vehicles screeched to a stop, a familiar voice cut through the air.

'THERE THEY ARE!' Dolly yelled, pointing towards Cos and her friends. She was surrounded by the other girls. Following them were a grimacing Detective Constable

Wensleydale and a frazzled-looking Miss Seymour.

'TOLD YOU WE WEREN'T LYING!'

A whimper escaped the Spectre's throat.

'You've been caught red-handed,' Aggie said fiercely. 'It's better to give yourself up.'

'Never,' hissed Miss Fox. She plunged her gloved hand into the pocket of Gideon Luminaire's white fur cloak and drew out a small glass bottle. Ripping off the stopper, she threw the bottle to the ground. But, instead of a huge cloud of smoke, a mere wisp escaped from the bottle. Cos realised that Miss Fox had planned to vanish in a puff of smoke, but the Amazing Luminaire's uselessness as an illusionist had thwarted her.

Fear flashed across the Spectre's face. She scowled at the magician, her teeth bared. 'You incompetent—'

But before she could finish her insult, a red-faced

Detective Constable Wensleydale had grabbed her by the wrist. 'Miss Fox? I think you have some questions to answer down at the station.'

THE LONDON GAZETTE

17th March 1900 Price 2d

THE SPECTRE UNMASKED: *NOTORIOUS SWINDLER TAKEN INTO CUSTODY*

A lady known as Miss Emerald Fox was apprehended by police as the Spectacular burned to the ground last night. Miss Fox, who had numerous aliases and a storied criminal past, has confessed to being the Spectre, an infamous mastermind whose thefts had flummoxed investigators for years. Mr Edmund Deans, who was wrongly accused of being the Spectre, is expected to be released from jail imminently.

AGATHA DE LA DULCE APPOINTED FIRST FEMALE EDITOR ON FLEET STREET

Always at the forefront of progress, the London Gazette *is pleased to announce the appointment of one of the most exciting journalists of the day to its editorship. Miss Agatha de la Dulce has already proven herself to be a talented writer, and her new role as editor marks an important first for women. She replaces long-standing editor Mr Milner, who resigned on Friday after concerns were raised about his journalistic integrity in light of the paper's investigation into the man wrongly accused of being the Spectre. Miss de la Dulce has pledged to transform the* Gazette *into a thoroughly modern newspaper that will champion do-gooding and right wrongs.*

THE LADY INVALID

GIFTED TO THE NATION

Art dealers Vincent & Sons have kindly donated a priceless Van Hackenboeck portrait to the National Gallery in London. Deemed an artwork of national importance, The Lady Invalid *was due to be auctioned off for what was predicted to be a record-breaking sum, but it will now go on permanent display to the general public, free of charge.*

EPILOGUE
A few days later

The Home thrummed with nervous anticipation. All evidence of the reverse heist was hidden away: Pearl's elaborate costumes for the Midnight Masquerade were carefully stowed, Diya's invention station had been cleared of all heist-helping contraptions and Mary had returned the stacks of books she'd used to plot their caper to their designated shelves in the library. Cos drummed her fingers against the armrest of her Wonderful Wheelchair, her gaze trained on the front door.

The girls and Miles had gathered on the comfy armchairs and sofas scattered about the entrance foyer. All were dressed in their best. They'd already had one false alarm that morning: when Dolly had skipped happily through the front door after delivering the package containing the

Siraj elephant to the post office.

The newly adopted Home cat weaved between their ankles, rubbing up against hands and handing out nose boops at every turn. Gideon Luminaire's allergies meant he couldn't keep her, and the girls had fallen in love with the intrepid feline – who, in Cos's opinion, had saved the day by knocking the Spectre's gun from her hand. There had been a fierce discussion about what to call her – after all, the Spectre had named her Cat, and it was unthinkable that she retain that moniker. After many suggestions, ideas and arguments, the girls, Miles, Miss Meriton and Aggie had finally agreed on the perfect name for an animal who prized exploring above all else: Scout. The newly christened Scout was thriving with her new family and enjoying chin scratches and treats aplenty.

But today, unusually, the Star Diamond Home was absent of noise: the laughter and chatter had been replaced by a tension-filled quiet.

'How much longer do you think she'll be?' Miles's voice punctured the silence. He loosened his firework-embroidered bow tie and undid the top button of his shirt. 'I'm missing my paint-splattered trousers.'

Miss Meriton paced back and forth across the entrance foyer. 'Not long now, Miles. Miss Seymour graciously gave us the weekend to recover after Friday's events, and wrote that her inspection would commence first thing Monday.' She smiled warmly at the children, but the evidence of her time as a captive of the Spectre was still etched across her hollow cheeks and pale face. She fiddled nervously with the silver band on her ring finger.

A nervous murmur rumbled throughout the building. Cos knew that they were all dreading the visit from the Inspectorate of Children's Institutions – especially after what had happened the last time Miss Seymour visited.

After Cos, Miles, Mary, Diya and Pearl had left for the Masquerade, the girls had given the inspector a tour of the Home. It had all gone swimmingly – until the fake matron's head suddenly toppled and rolled on the floor towards Miss Seymour's feet. Miss Seymour had screeched, and only after a grovelling letter from the real Miss Meriton had she been persuaded to redo her inspection.

Cos cringed every time she thought of it. Their happiness, and the wonderful home they had created together, hinged on the outcome of this inspection. If Miss Seymour thought the Star Diamond Home was failing to educate them properly, the Inspectorate would fire Miss Meriton, the Home would be shut down and the girls could be scattered to institutions across the country, far from their friends and family. It was an awful possibility. And, given how displeased the inspector had been when she'd discovered their ever-so-slight embellishment of the truth, Cos wasn't sure how likely it was that the Home would get a glowing review.

But an even bigger worry pressed heavily on Cos. Ever since Friday evening, when the girls had found the stolen items *and* proved that the lady known as Miss Fox was the Spectre, Cos had been impatiently waiting for her father to be released from jail. Given that even the police had accepted he was an innocent man framed by the villain, Edmund should have been released immediately. But to Cos's disgust there were lengthy and boring procedures that had to be gone through first. As soon as she'd had a restorative cup of tea, Aggie had marched down to the jail, armed with her never-ending determination to right wrongs, only to be told that Cos's father would have to go before a judge to secure his liberty. Undeterred, Aggie had spent her weekend flitting from the jail, to the police station, to the courthouse – but to no avail. Edmund had spent a few more nights in his cold, cheerless cell.

Cos had been racked with guilt over her inability to help. Their shenanigans at the Midnight Masquerade had triggered a flare-up in her disability. Her limbs were full of pain, her brain was caught in a swirl of fog that made it difficult to concentrate and she'd dislocated a thumb and a knee over the weekend. Miss Meriton and Aggie had told her in no uncertain terms that she was not to do anything remotely reckless – like, say, break her father out of prison. She was to stay at home and rest.

But now Monday morning was upon them, and Aggie had headed to court first thing. Cos's stomach twisted painfully. She felt – not for the first time – as though she were split in half. Part of her felt as if she ought to speed-wheel to the court and demand her dad's freedom. But the other half wanted to help Miss Meriton and all her friends save their Home. As these thoughts fought inside her, their battle was interrupted by a short, sharp rap on the door.

Cos's stomach somersaulted. Miss Meriton let out a long-held breath, smoothed her already perfect hair and strode towards the door. The children tried to arrange themselves neatly, all plastering welcoming smiles upon their faces. The door opened, revealing a pursed-lipped, prune-faced lady clutching a clipboard. *Miss Seymour*. Her beady eyes scanned the entrance foyer, her expression unsmiling. There was still a rather large bump on her forehead.

'Miss Seymour!' Miss Meriton forced a nervous grin. 'Welcome to the Star Diamond Home for Girls.'

The inspector's sensible shoes *click-clacked* as she stepped inside. 'Hmmph.'

Cos sighed. Miss Seymour was going to be a tough nut to crack, especially after their earlier interactions. They were going to have to pull out all the stops if they were going to charm Miss Seymour. But, if anyone could do it, it was them.

Miss Seymour left the Home an hour later, a woman transformed. She waved a cheery goodbye to the girls, her scowl replaced by a beam. Pearl had speedily created a fashionable hat for the inspector, coloured a rather fetching shade of lilac. Mary had devised a simple yet effective template for Miss Seymour to write up her inspections. Diya had invented a clipboard visor so that the inspector could take notes even in the brightest of sunlight. And Miles had unpicked a clasp on Miss Seymour's bag that had been stuck fast for months. Even Scout had played her part – the inspector had pronounced her 'the most handsome feline'.

'That was *spectacular*,' Diya muttered out of the corner of her mouth.

'Maybe our greatest caper yet,' added Mary.

'Much more audacious than a jewel heist,' agreed Miles. '*And* a reverse art heist.'

Miss Meriton clutched the piece of paper that Miss Seymour had handed her as she departed. It said that the Star Diamond Home for Girls was a more than acceptable environment in which to raise children. Relief flickered across the matron's face. All her hard work had been worth it.

'Well, after that I think we deserve a treat,' she said. 'Tea and cake it is!'

A cheer went up from the residents of the Home, but as the others excitedly rushed to the kitchen Cos's thoughts drifted back to her father. She peered into the street, willing Aggie and Edmund to appear like magic. Instead the world seemed to go on as normal: two doors down, old Miss Calvert was busy airing her latest fabric swatches by the door of her haberdashery shop, Mr Willis was passing copies of the latest edition of the *London Gazette* to his newsboy and Londoners strolled by, enjoying the spring sunshine.

Pearl placed a gentle arm across her shoulders. 'He'll be all right, Cos.'

Cos laid her head on her friend's shoulder. She hoped Pearl was right.

Mary stepped forward to close the door, shutting away the bustle of the outside. 'Aggie won't let us down, Cos. And woe betide the judge who disagrees with her – she's like a fire-breathing dragon when she's got a cause she believes in.'

Cos tried to nod, but tears welled in her eyes and her words caught in her throat.

'Come on,' Diya said softly, nodding towards the kitchen. Laughter spilled out from the room. 'Let's help with the baking – it'll take your mind off everything.'

Cos rolled into the kitchen, following her friends. Steam curled up from the spout of the kettle as Dolly carefully lined up twenty mugs on the side. At the other kitchen counter, a storm of flour had been scattered about, dusting hair and noses in a smattering of white. Miss Meriton and the girls gathered round a humongous mixing bowl and measuring scales, jostling each other as they all strained to help make the cake.

'Cos!' Miss Meriton said, holding out a wooden spoon. 'Want to stir?'

But as Cos reached for the spoon there was a knock at the door.

A familiar duo stood in the doorway. Aggie wore, as always, a determined expression, tendrils of curls escaping from her up-do. Edmund's hair had been closely cropped, and he looked far thinner than Cos remembered. But he was smiling in that starry twinkling way Cos had come to love. Her breath hitched in her throat.

Aggie grinned, locking eyes with Miss Meriton, who shrieked in a most unlike-Miss-Meriton way and ran towards the journalist, pulling her into a hug.

'DAD!' Cos was wheeling towards Edmund before her brain had even registered what was happening. She collided with him – a little more fiercely than she'd intended – and wrapped her arms round him. She only realised she was crying when she felt that her cheeks were wet.

Cos sniffed away her tears as she pulled away, staring into her dad's face. She grabbed his sewing kit and unclasped the chain round her neck, handing both items back to their rightful owner. 'Are you all right?'

'I'm all right,' he promised. 'But this is yours now.' He pressed the locket back into Cos's palm. 'It's what Mina would've wanted.'

'Oh, Cos,' Aggie said. Cos noticed that her fingers were intertwined with Miss Meriton's.

Before Cos could say or do anything else, Dolly ran towards her, engulfing Cos and her dad in another squeeze. Then Ida did the same. Before she knew it, Cos and her dad were at the centre of a gigantic group hug, which quickly descended into a giggling tangle of girls and Miles.

Hugs, thought Cos, *were* spectacular.

Acknowledgements

I am thrilled, delighted and honestly a little surprised to be joining the second-book club! This book was by far the hardest and most rewarding thing I have ever written, and I'm so excited for it to be in your hands.

My first thanks has to go to my agent, Lydia Silver, whose enthusiasm and support for me and my writing has never wavered, even when I was convinced I was the worst writer ever. I'm as proud as ever to work with you and the whole lovely Darley Anderson Children's Team.

My HarperCollins Children's Books family – I am so lucky to work with such an incredible team of talented and hardworking people. My wonderful acquiring editor, Michelle Misra, for her passion and care. My equally amazing new editor Nat, who has been a dream to work with. Your excellent editorial notes and gentle encouragement helped transform Cos 2 into the story I wanted to tell. A huge thank you to Nick Lake and Cally Poplak for their championing of Cos from the get go, Jane Baldock and Jane Hammett for polishing my words to perfection and untangling my timeline— apologies for my obsession with the em-dash. To my incredible PR and marketing team present and past: Charlotte Winstone, Ellie Curtis, Sarah Lough and Jess Dean. Thank you all for being on Team Cos! To Flavia Sorrentino for the stunning cover and interior illustrations, and to Elorine Grant and Matthew Kelly for interior and cover design.

My family and friends have been, as always, incredibly

supportive whilst I wrestled my words into the shape of a book. I love you all so much. Special mention must go to Marnie Calvert and the newly minted Gladwell-Ashers – thank you for letting me steal your names to put in my book. To Kate Jakubiak, thank you for slotting so perfectly into the Noakes chaos.

Booksellers, librarians and book bloggers are some of the best people I have ever met. In the past year they have spread the word about Cos and I am eternally grateful for that. Particular thanks to the superstars at Waterstones Carlisle and Bookends, and to Debbie at Potton Library.

I had a bit of a tricky health time whilst writing this book. Dealing with a lifelong disability is hard sometimes, and trying to write on top of that was, at times, impossible. I am, as ever, in awe of our NHS and aware of just how important it is to safeguard it for future generations. I'm also so thankful to disability specific organisations: Ehlers-Danlos Support UK and The Ehlers-Danlos Society have been particularly supportive to both me and Cos.

To the readers, no words can adequately express just how much every single one of you mean to me. Every email, every social media post, every 'I like your book!' means the absolute world to me. Thank you for taking my swear-y, impulsive girl to your hearts.

Finally: thank you to my husband, Connor, my best friend, partner and co-cat parent. You, Scout and Sunny are my absolute world.